The Franklin Boys' Story: Sunset, Sunrise

Editor: Jessica McLeod

Cover art: Taylor Watkins

Headshot: Rachel Yeomans of Rachel Yeomans Media

Dedication

I would like to dedicate this book to the many high schoolers out there who have overcome tragedy in their lives and come out on the other end. Over the years, I have run into so many inspirational young people. To those young people out there who on a daily basis face tragedy through the loss of a loved one, thoughts about suicide, knowing someone involved in drugs, or facing racism, always remember there is someone who loves you and cares about you. From the start you were the inspiration for this story. Always remember after every Sunset there is always a Sunrise. Lastly, I'd like to thank my friend and fellow teacher, Patty Mann, who pushed me and constantly inspired me to be a better teacher.

Acknowledgement

When I started my writing journey I never really expected to write one, much less, three books. I could have never done it without the support of my friends and family. I would like to give a special thanks to my editor, Jessica, for her tireless work and support. Lastly, I would like to give a special thanks to my students. Without them the desire to tell their story would have been greatly diminished.

1

Coach Jacobs

Early July

Jeremy pulled into the Franklin Memorial Cemetery. With the day coming to an end, the sun was partly hidden by the trees. Jeremy paused and glanced in every direction. There wasn't a car in sight and the cemetery was silent except for the crickets which seemingly surrounded the area with their noisy songs.

At first he couldn't remember where Jamie was buried. It had been several months since he had last visited her grave. With a red rose in one hand and a tube of cherry lipstick in the other hand, he walked quietly across the scattered gravel, which crunched under his feet, towards Jamie's gravestone. Once he reached her grave, he silently knelt. One lonely tear ran down his cheek.

Eventually, the one tear fell from his face and onto the folded handwritten note he held in his right hand.

Dear Jamie,

I miss you. I miss your smile. I'll never forget the first time you said hello to me. Between you and me our first kiss is etched in my mind. Believe it or not, you were the first girl I've ever kissed. Sorry if I wasn't very good at it. I can't help but smile when I think about the day we won state and I noticed you excitedly jumping up and down on the bleachers.

I'm sorry I didn't hear your calls for help. I'm sorry I wasn't a better friend. I'm not mad at you and I hope you're not mad at me.

Jamie, I'm confused. Should I go on with my life or am I supposed to be sad forever? Damn, I miss you! People always say, you don't know what you have until it's gone. I never fully understood that statement until your death. Others miss you as well, but I'm sure you know that as you look down on us from heaven. Even Cali misses you. I know you two were like oil and water but she sure does miss you.

Please help me feel your presence. Help me move on. I'm so confused.

You'll always be in my heart because you were my first love.

Love, Jeremy

P.S. Here's a tube of cherry lipstick and a rose for you. The cherry lipstick is for the first time you kissed me, and the rose is for my eternal love.

Besides Jeremy, Jamie was one of those super amazing kids. Jamie was a fighter until she sadly couldn't fight anymore. She was a sophomore when she committed suicide. Sadly, the poor girl couldn't find her place in Franklin. Just when we thought she had reached rock bottom, she turned things around… or so we thought. Yeah, I wish I or the other teachers at Franklin High School would've heard her calls for help. I know Jeremy wishes he had.

Mentally tired, Jeremy rolled on to his butt and rested against Jamie's gravestone. He stared to his right and noticed the orange tinted sky which appeared slightly above the trees. Strangely enough, he didn't notice the colors in the early evening sky until that moment. A couple of trees swayed back and forth in the breeze. Quietly, he contemplated whether to attend college or go pro, like his brother. Brandy, a long time friend of Jeremy's, crossed his mind.

Brandy was there for Jeremy when Jamie died. After all, Jeremy was there for her when the roles had been reversed. Yeah, it was a pretty rough spring for the two of them. In many ways, they were the only ones who could relate to each other after such a traumatic spring.

We weren't sure if four months was enough time to have properly healed, much less them date. Some of the girls thought Brandy was a bitch, while others were simply against Brandy and Jeremy dating because he was African American. Franklin was, after all, a racist town for the longest time. It took people like Jeremy and his brother to break down some of the barriers. Still, some people in Franklin remained backwards in their thinking. I guess you can't change everyone.

As one of Jeremy's baseball coaches, I was a little shocked with the racist beliefs that existed in Franklin. I guess I shouldn't have been because southern Illinois towns were notoriously racist, but that was back in the 60s and I moved to Franklin in the 2000s. Before coming to Franklin to teach P.E., I played minor league baseball for the St. Louis Cardinals. When I realized playing in the major leagues was not going to happen, I gave it up and went into teaching. After teaching and coaching in a small town just outside of St. Louis, I moved to Franklin to teach and coach. While teaching in Franklin, I was lucky enough to coach and teach a lot of amazing young men and women.

A Monarch butterfly rested on Jeremy's knee. The butterfly's speckled wings managed to make Jeremy smile. It fluttered its delicate wings several times. He wanted to touch the beautiful creature, but he was afraid of hurting it.

As if it overstayed its welcome, the butterfly seemingly leapt from Jeremy's knee and danced in the air. He followed it with his eyes until it eventually disappeared.

Jeremy turned and looked at Jamie's gravestone. "Jamie...I love you. I'll never forget you. You'll always be a part of my life."

He laid the rose, the tube of cherry lipstick, and the folded note up next to the gravestone.

Quietly, he stared at the grave. Finally, he stood up.

With his right hand, he wiped away the one tear from his cheek. He turned and quietly walked away. Jeremy had nothing more to say.

2

Coach Jacobs

Late June

Brandy couldn't stop smiling as she and Jeremy zoomed down the southern Illinois highway. Corn and soybean fields were scattered throughout the area. Rolling hills covered with trees could be seen just beyond the fields. To their left, the sun slowly crept below the trees.

Jeremy glanced at her and smiled.

Brandy looked back at Jeremy.

"What?" she asked playfully while slapping him on the leg.

"Ah, nothing."

"No, really, what?" she asked again.

"Well, I'm just glad we're out tonight. Is that okay?"

Brandy squeezed his leg.

"I'm glad you asked me out. It took you long enough, you big dork."

Jeremy's smile disappeared as he shrugged his shoulders.

"Yeah, well the timing wasn't right I guess."

"Oh well, you finally did, and I'm glad you did." Brandy poked him on the leg. "You look amazing in that shirt by the way. I love your arms."

Thankful for the compliment, Jeremy shyly smiled.

The two remained quiet for several more minutes. Any

sort of conversation would've been nearly impossible because the front car windows were down.

"So..." Brandy asked with a pause as they pulled up to a stop light. "...where are we going?"

"It's a surprise," he said with a sly grin.

"Ohhh a surprise? I love surprises!" Brandy replied while giggling.

Finally, they arrived at Jeremy's favorite pizza place located in Carbondale. Of course, Brandy was no stranger to the place. She figured this was the destination but she didn't have the heart to tell him and ruin "the big surprise."

Throughout the evening the two ate, talked, and laughed. Neither of them had done much laughing the prior few months, so it felt good. She especially loved the way Jeremy made her giggle at the dumbest things.

The two pulled out of the parking lot and headed back towards Franklin. A few miles down the road Brandy yelled, "Dude, stop here!"

She frantically pointed to her right. She loved going to the coffee shop in Carbondale. She was very much like Alexa, who was a friend of Brandy's and the girlfriend of Julio, Jeremy's brother. Alexa was originally from California and at the moment she was attending Stanford University. Jeremy pushed on the brakes which nearly caused the car behind theirs to collide into them.

"There's nowhere to park!" Brandy exclaimed as they pulled into the parking lot.

Apparently there were others besides Brandy who had coffee on the brain.

Like an eagle in search of its prey, Jeremy continued to look for a parking space.

"Oh wait...there's a place up ahead!" she yelled enthusiastically.

Jeremy didn't have the heart to inform her he had seen the space already. He didn't want to ruin her excitement.

The car rolled to a stop. Brandy cheerfully slugged Jeremy on the arm. "This is my treat."

Though Jeremy wasn't a coffee drinker, a cool lemonade sounded good. After ordering their drinks, they walked back towards the car.

She noticed Jeremy had a strange look on his face as she sipped her drink through the long straw. "What's up? What's wrong?"

"*Iced* coffee, that's strange."

He paused.

"I didn't know you drank *iced* coffee. That's news to me. Heck, I've never seen Alexa drink iced coffee and she drinks coffee ALL the time."

Amused, Brandy smiled. "I guess you have an education ahead of you then, buster. If you're going to spend time with me, that is."

With their hands clasped the two walked towards Jeremy's car at the pace a turtle could've kept up with. The cloudless southern Illinois sky allowed them to notice every star God had created. The whole time home Brandy kept her window down. After a long day in the summer heat, the cool air felt good on her skin, even if it made her long brunette hair whip around. While they passed the corn fields and rolling countryside hills, the two continued to quietly smile.

3

Coach Jacobs

Late June

With Julio living in San Francisco, texting was Jeremy's main way of communicating with him. Jeremy would also browse the internet every few days to see if Julio had recently pitched. He wasn't a starter yet, so his appearances were sporadic in nature. Every once in a while, Jeremy would even send me a text.

Hey Coach, did you see Julio pitched last night

...Or something to that effect. Sometimes Jeremy would sit on his bed or on the living room couch and imagine playing in the pros against his brother.

As a present to his brother, Julio bought Jeremy a big screen TV. Julio also bought his family a cable subscription, even though his parents could afford it. He bought it so they could watch all the professional baseball games they wanted to watch.

Two days after Jeremy and Brandy's evening out, Jeremy was up in his room watching a game when his phone buzzed.

You free this evening, dinner on me. Picking you up

at 6, okay?

He paused. Instead of texting her back, he pressed the call button on his phone.

Finally, after several rings, she picked up her phone.

"Hey Jeremy… So are you able to go out tonight?"

Stretched out on his bed and looking up towards the ceiling, Jeremy responded happily. "Yeah, I'm free. Where are we going?"

"Geeze, a girl asks you out and you get all nosey. Man!" She responded jokingly.

Jeremy laughed. "Okay… Okay. I'll be ready by 6." He paused. "I'm assuming you're picking me up as well?"

"You need to work on your listening skills. Didn't I just say I'm taking YOU out?!"

"Uh, yeah."

"Okay then, you goober, I'll be there around 6!"

Jeremy hung up his phone and laid motionless on his bed for several minutes like a slug. For better or worse, he couldn't help but notice the contrast in personalities between Brandy and Jamie. Brandy had a special quality about her. She made him laugh.

Between the warm temperatures, high humidity, and having no clue where they were going, Jeremy decided wearing khaki shorts and a blue collared shirt was his best move.

He was nearly ready when he heard her pull into the driveway. Excited, he looked at himself in his bathroom mirror to make sure everything was in order. He spritzed himself with his favorite cologne, bound down the stairs, and ran towards the front door as if he was in a race. She walked energetically up the steps of the front porch. Before she was able to ring the doorbell, he swung the door open.

"Wow!" she declared, "You look amazing!"

"Oh, shut up," he replied shyly. "I should be complimenting you!"

Flattered, Brandy flashed him a smile as she flipped her hair to her right side. "Are you ready to go?!"

For some reason, he had never noticed her irresistible dimples. She guided him down the steps with her hand. Her playful enthusiasm energized him.

"So where are we going?" he asked as they got into her car.

She playfully shrugged her shoulders.

"I dunno."

Jeremy leaned against the car door. His arm dangled out the car window as they rode through town. The breeze felt good, even though it felt like he was in a blast furnace.

"Brandy… can I ask you a question?"

"Yeah, just as long as it's not where we're going." Her response was rather emphatic.

"I always thought you were pretty, but why do you seem prettier the more times we get together?"

Brandy smiled. "Oh yeah? Maybe it's because of the capris and pink top I have on... or maybe, just maybe, because I'm just growing on yah?"

She slowed the car down as they approached the entrance to the local park. At the entrance stood an old statue of the former senator, Stephen A Douglas. The statue was surrounded by a number of picnic tables. Woods surrounded the park, while a small stream wound along the edge of the park and eventually fed into the Mississippi river several miles away.

Brandy quickly jumped out of the car. Jeremy, confused, remained inside.

"Dork, I made you supper!"

The two looked around the park not quite sure where to go, even though the park was completely empty. Jeremy was new to the picnic experience, at least with a girl his age. All of the other times were with his parents and all of those times he just followed his parents around like a duck. A picnic with a girl was definitely new territory. Embarrassingly, Brandy didn't know where to sit either, so they stood next to the car waiting on the other to take the lead.

Finally, after looking around the park, Brandy took command. She nudged him with her elbow and pointed towards a table under a large oak tree about fifteen feet from the car. Next to the oak tree stood several cherry trees which caught Brandy's attention.

Jeremy reached for the basket of food.

"Let me carry this," he said, surprising her in a good way.

Time passed quickly while they enjoyed the dinner Brandy had fixed. The birds sang happily to each other. Several of the birds playfully flew up and around the oak tree. Others sat on the branches of the cherry trees. When there was a pause in the conversation, Brandy would look away and listen to the birds.

She nervously looked at Jeremy.

"So, I have some news to share with you."

He put down the drumstick he was in the process of devouring.

"What's up?"

She reached for his hand.

"Well I got accepted into CIU today. I know we have a year until graduation, but this is the school I've always wanted to attend."

Jeremy smiled.

"That's awesome! I didn't even know you were applying there."

"Well, I'm not surprised. You were a little consumed this past spring, as was I, but I actually applied back in February."

"Quite honestly, I've been looking at schools in the area

and Central Illinois has been one of those schools. What do you think about that, Missy?"

"I love it! Oh, in a week I'm going up to Champaign to visit the campus with my parents for the day. Do you want to join us? I'm sure they wouldn't mind. Heck, my parents think the world of you."

"Sounds like a great idea. Let me mention it to my parents first, though."

The birds soon gave way to the crickets as the sun began to set. A few birds continued to sing to each other, but the numbers were definitely fewer than before. The sun soon gave way to the night. As the two walked happily back to the car, several mosquitoes dive bombed them.

Jeremy sat comfortably in the car seat. He was waiting for Brandy to get herself organized when his phone buzzed. Curious, Jeremy checked his phone.

"Huh, it's a text from my brother" he said out loud.

"Oh yeah, what's it say? Open it up."

Jeremy clicked on the read button.

Threw 8 innings, only allowed 2 runs

Overwhelmed with pride, Jeremy clenched his fist and pumped it up and down several times. He leaned over and kissed Brandy on the cheek.

4

Luke Fisher

Late June

Throughout much of the spring, the fans packed the stadium in support of our team. We were neck and neck with our divisional rival, the Dodgers. Every game grew in importance as we crept into summer.

Alright, you may be asking, 'who in the heck is this guy?' Right? Well my name is Luke Fisher. Julio and I were drafted a year ago by the San Francisco Giants. We quickly worked our way through the minor league farm system. I was drafted out of college, the University of Florida more specifically, while Julio was drafted right out of high school after he had won the State Championship for the tiny town of Franklin.

It was quite a ride. In our first summer in the majors, I actually became the starting center fielder while Julio still waited for his big chance to earn a spot in the pitching rotation. The guy was tall, threw the ball hard, and was built like a brick house.

Julio and I became good friends in the process.

Prior to one of our many road trips, the team had a mid afternoon game, which wasn't common, but welcomed every once in a while. Julio settled into his spot in the bullpen where relief pitchers sat during the game.

"Well boys, another easy day for us with Gordon on the mound," muttered one of the relief pitchers as our team took the field.

Pitchers throughout the league hated pitching against the Dodgers. They were one of the best hitting teams in our league, with plenty of power up and down the lineup. The game started with two routine ground balls to the shortstop for outs. Then, on the first pitch to the third batter, I noticed Gordon rubbing his arm. *That's no good*, I thought to myself.

Gordon's next pitch was God awful. After the pitch, he rotated his arm clockwise and then counterclockwise. *Oh crap, this isn't good at all*, I said to myself. I couldn't imagine what he was thinking at the time.

Ole Gordon walked around to the back of the mound. In frustration he rested his hands on his hips. I could only see his back, but I could tell he wasn't happy. I went to one knee out in centerfield, when I noticed the trainer walk briskly from the dugout to the mound.

The manager, Carl Smith, leapt from the bench. He was just steps behind the trainer.

"What's the problem here?" Carl asked in a gruff upon reaching the mound.

"Well... it appears Gordon has hurt his shoulder," replied John Jackson, the trainer.

Coach Smith looked at Gordon.

"So what happened?"

"On the first pitch to this batter, I felt a pull in my shoulder. I tried one more pitch but it hurt even more."

Carl Smith looked towards the bullpen located just beyond the outfield fence.

He looked at the pitching coach, Frank Sims who was standing on the field next to Coach Smith. "Who should we go with?"

Frank took a deep breath.

"Julio."

"Well shit, get Julio up and throwing then. Dammit!" Coach Smith demanded.

Seconds later the bullpen phone rang.

"Julio… get up and throw!" yelled the bullpen coach.

Julio took a breath, gathered his thoughts, and began to get loose. After he quickly stretched, he sprinted onto the field.

Finally, he was loose and ready to pitch. Coach Smith stood on the edge of the dugout steps. He looked at his trusted pitching coach and then back towards the field.

"Frank, do you think he can go extended time tonight?"

Coach Sims was an old school coach. He loved to swear, yell, and chew tobacco. Man, he was a blast to be around … as long as the swearing wasn't directed at you. Most importantly, he knew how to get the very best out of his pitchers, which was one of the reasons why we were so good.

Frank looked at Carl. "Relax, if anyone can go six to seven innings, it's Julio. If he can't, well then, we're in trouble." He didn't even use one swear word. What a surprise!

The third batter weakly grounded out to second base for the last out of the inning. With his head down, Julio walked towards the dugout. Gordon stood at the edge of the dugout and awaited Julio's arrival. Like a proud father greeting his son, Gordon yelled out "go get'em, bud."

Julio tipped his cap and mouthed the word "thanks." He quietly walked to the farthest part of the dugout in search of some solitude. While we were at bat, I walked over and sat down next to him. Though he did his best to ignore me, my winning smile got the best of him.

"What the heck are you smiling about?"

I slapped him on the knee. "Mow 'em down bud, this game is yours."

I stood up and walked away before he had a chance to respond. If anyone knew the magnitude of this game for Julio, it was me. The last thing he wanted to do was fail miserably, assuring himself a lifetime of relief pitching if he was lucky. I had a feeling he was nervous as shit.

By the seventh inning we took the lead. All of the fans were on their feet in support of their young pitcher. Every time the opposition made an out they cheered. Imagine 40,000 people wearing burnt orange and black and standing and cheering. Yeah, it was pretty cool, especially from the outfield.

As we headed into the eighth inning, Coach Smith tapped his pitching coach on the leg.

"Assuming he gets through this inning, should we get someone up?"

Coach Sims let out a laugh that sounded like a damn machine gun.

"Uh, yeah," he said without hesitation.

"Well get the bullpen up and throwing then. Let's shut the door on them. Damn!" Smith responded impatiently.

Finally, the last out of the eighth inning came with a weak fly to me in center field. As he watched the final out of the inning drift into my glove, Julio pumped his fist several times. Though he was probably tired, adrenaline was surely running through his veins. He was on top of the pitching mountaintop. Hell, I'm sure he could've pitched seven more innings had they asked him too.

Julio made his way towards the dugout. He was greeted by Coach Smith. Coach reached out his hand.

"Great game, Julio, but you're done for the night. Grab a seat and relax."

He was disappointed but realistic. Julio passed through the dugout in search of his quiet spot. As he walked through the dugout many of the players congratulated him. Finally, he found his spot in the farthest corner of the dugout. He was probably in search of a little peace as he watched the game finish out.

Going into the ninth inning, Charlie Wigs was called on to end the game. He had become one of the most dominating closers in the league. He rarely blew a save.

From the field Charlie looked at Julio.

"Don't worry rookie. I've got this!" he confidently exclaimed over the loud music.

I loved it when Charlie came in to pitch. The stadium played a series of raucous heavy metal tunes, which got every fan up and onto their feet.

The first batter flew out to me in centerfield. One down. Julio sat on the bench and pumped his fist. Two more outs to go!

The next batter lazily grounded out to second base. The crowd was super loud by now. So loud chills went down my spine.

Charlie quickly had two strikes on the next batter. Julio couldn't sit any longer. He stood up and cheered like the rest of the team. Charlie reared back and threw a hard fastball by the batter for strike three. As soon as the umpire motioned strike three, Julio gleefully ran onto the field.

Excited, I ran towards the infield to congratulate Julio. As soon as I reached the jubilant rookie, I threw my arms around him.

"It's about time you do something worthwhile for this team," I said sarcastically.

Julio smiled. This was his moment and I was sure proud of him.

The two of us walked towards the dugout when Coach Smith stopped us.

"Well look at the two rookies." He looked at Julio. "Plan on pitching in five days. You've just earned yourself a starting slot."

Julio nodded. "Yes sir, thank you sir."

After several reporters stopped Julio to ask him about the game, he walked into the clubhouse. He immediately searched through his locker for his phone, which was buried in his clothes.

Once he found his phone, he quickly looked for Jeremy's number.

His fingers energetically pressed on his phone.

Threw 8 innings, only allowed 2 runs

After he sent a text to Jeremy he searched for Alexa's number. Excitedly, he typed:

I thew 8 inings toniht and won!

He was so excited typos riddled his text to Alexa, which made her giggle when she received it. I texted Pam, my girlfriend, the outcome as well. I was, after all, excited for the guy.

I looked at him as I got dressed. I don't think the guy stopped smiling. It was a big win for him.

5

Coach Jacobs

Late June

Jeremy felt a smack on his arm. Startled, he glanced at Brandy.

"You okay? Man, you had the cheesiest grin on your face."

"Nah... a lot is on my mind. It's all good. I'm still trying to figure out why you had to hit me though...bully."

"You game for a coke or something?" she asked, hoping he was in no rush to go home.

Even though he was curious if his parents had heard about Julio's outing against the Dodgers, he had no desire to go home so soon.

"I would love a coke," he replied.

Their arms swung back and forth as they walked up Brandy's driveway towards her house like a couple of second graders.

They stopped several feet in front of her house. A street light shined down on the two like a spot light in a play.

"So what are you thinking about?" she asked stubbornly.

"Sorry, I'm just excited for Julio."

Brandy let go of his hand and clasped onto his left arm with both hands. She pulled herself towards him and ran her fingers lovingly up and down his arm.

"I know you are babe. That will be you in a few years. I know it."

"You think?" he asked, somewhat unsure of himself.

"Of course, babe. You got game," she added proudly.

Jeremy laughed out loud. "Well, I appreciate your confidence in me."

She smacked him on the arm, again. "Nah, you know you're going to go far. I hope to be there with you every step of the way."

Jeremy laughed again. "I just hope you don't get too tired of me."

They eventually made their way to the back of the house. Again, they found themselves in the middle of a spotlight. While they sat on the porch couch, Brandy nestled her head onto Jeremy's arm and listened to the crickets sing their love songs. Her hair flowed off her back and onto the porch couch.

"I could lay here all night," she whispered as she kissed him on the arm.

Jeremy repositioned his body, careful not to move her head. Quietly, the two sat on the couch when a bustling at the back door caught their attention.

Out stepped Brandy's mom. The resemblance between Brandy and her mom was quite uncanny.

"Hey kids! Sorry to disrupt you, but I thought you'd like something to drink," she said softly.

Being the presumptuous mom she was, she held out two glasses filled with soda and ice, which clanked as she walked.

Brandy worked her way up from her side position and leaned up against Jeremy.

"Thanks Mom."

Though Brandy was appreciative of the drinks, she was slightly upset that her mom disrupted her quiet time with Jeremy.

Brandy's mom set the two glasses down on the table in front of the couch. She looked at the two and half heartedly smiled.

"Brandy...dear...did you ask Jeremy if he wanted to visit CIU with us?"

Aggravated and slightly embarrassed, Brandy replied with a long, drawn out, "Mommmmmmm!"

Humored, Jeremy playfully nudged Brandy several times in her right side, Brandy continued to look at her mom, un-humored by Jeremy's exploits. She didn't respond to her mom's question, but instead sat quietly next to Jeremy hoping her mom would disappear back into the house. Unmoved by her daughter's desires, her mom stood at the door and waited for an answer.

Finally, ready for her mom to re-enter the house, Brandy responded.

"We talked about it briefly tonight."

"Oh good." Mrs. Jackson looked at Jeremy. "We're hoping to go next week sometime. We plan on leaving early and coming back the same day."

Jeremy smiled. "Thanks Mrs. Jackson, I appreciate the invite. It means a lot."

"No problem, Jeremy," she said with a grin. "Well, I don't want to bother you kids, so I'll let you be."

Brandy looked at Jeremy in agony after her mom went back into the house.

"Man, my mom can be such a nag," she said in disgust. Jeremy reached for his drink, slightly amused by Brandy's reaction towards her mom.

"Nah, she just cares about you. Your mom is no different than most of the moms out there."

Brandy's eyes widened. "You can't be serious. My mom is such a pain! Ugg!"

A few minutes quietly passed. Jeremy glanced at his phone and realized it was nearly midnight. Brandy resumed her previous position by pressing her head up against Jeremy's arm while her legs were stretched out on the couch. Her chest rose and fell with every breath. Jeremy leaned over and kissed her on the head. At peace, she flashed him a small grin.

"I have to go," he said with regret.

"No, I don't want you to go," she sleepily muttered.

"Sorry, but I have to."

"Alright, if you have to," she replied as she rolled her bottom lip.

Brandy begrudgingly sat up. He leaned over and gave her a soft kiss on the lips. To his delight, her pouty face all but disappeared.

Jeremy stood up and stretched himself out. He bent over and put his right hand underneath her chin. She closed her eyes in preparation for what she hoped would be a kiss. Never to disappoint her, he kissed her softly on the lips one last time.

Jeremy peeled himself away from Brandy. She remained nestled on the couch as he walked confidently to the front of the house.

6

Coach Jacobs

Early July

The day was early as the sun crept up over the horizon. For the most part, the interstate was empty except for the few truckers who seemed to hog the lanes and a few out of state cars.

In the back seat next to Jeremy sat Brandy. No matter how hard she tried, she couldn't stay awake. Thankfully, he got along with Brandy's parents, otherwise Jeremy would've had to pretend to be asleep.

He quietly sat in the back seat and watched their car pass the many corn and soybean fields. Her parents reminded him of his own. Both his and Brandy's parents trusted their kids, kept them inline, weren't pushy, and most importantly they didn't ask him too many questions.

The morning became increasingly warmer as they approached Champaign, where Central Illinois University, commonly known as CIU, is located. Brandy was wide awake and energized. So much so that she playfully poked Jeremy in his side a few times.

Champaign was like many midwestern towns. It was surrounded by fields as far as the eye could see with trees sparsely scattered in every direction. Every fall, the university doubled the size of Champaign from 30,000 to roughly 60,000. The dorms rose above the skyline and could be seen from miles away. Of course, it certainly helped that there were no hills of any relative size in central Illinois.

"Wow, there isn't as much traffic as I thought there'd be," declared Mr. Jackson. "Well, it's probably because it's summertime. In a few weeks, I bet it's busy."

Brandy rolled her eyes. "Okay, Mr. Know it all."

Her mom turned in her seat and glared at Brandy.

"Excuse me, but have you ever been to college?" she asked rhetorically.

"Uh, no," Brandy responded with a small attitude.

Poor Jeremy slumped against the window in hopes of staying out of the verbal gunfire.

Her mom lowered her sunglasses to the tip of her nose.

"Okay then, we don't need your commentary, is that understood young lady?"

"Yes ma'am," Brandy responded respectfully.

Brandy's frustration quickly subsided as they drove through campus.

The university wasn't surrounded by any major beach, beautiful forest, or mountain range. Instead, it was stuck in the middle of Illinois cornfields. It was certainly not an Ivy League school either, but it was one of the best in the region. The school was close, but not too close to Franklin. Brandy liked that. CIU also had an awesome engineering program, which was her interest.

Finally, they reached the Office of Admissions. The four peeled themselves out of the car. As soon as they got out, they all began to sweat because of the summer heat. Thankfully it was not even midmorning yet. Quickly, they walked towards the building entrance. Once inside, they immediately felt a rush of cool air upon their arms and face.

Mr. Jackson led the troop down the hall towards the Office of Admissions. Slightly behind him was his wife who had given up trying to walk next to him years ago, especially when he was on a mission. Brandy and Jeremy were several feet behind. They weren't in quite the hurry he was.

Finally, they reached a long set of windows which extended from the floor to the ceiling. In the middle stood a set of glass doors. The doors opened to an office where two college-aged girls worked. To the untrained eye, one would've thought the two were working diligently ... but it was summer after all. The one at the front desk smiled when they walked in.

"Can I help you?"

"Yes, my daughter and her boyfriend have a scheduled meeting with an advisor today," Mr. Jackson replied politely.

Boyfriend? Scheduled meeting? This was all news to Jeremy.

"You must be the Jacksons," the young lady said with a smile, as she brushed her long wavy hair to the side with her fingers. "We have you down. Go ahead and have a seat. She'll be with you in a few."

Not long after they sat down, a tall lean African-American woman walked around the corner. As soon as she rounded the corner of the office she flashed a smile.

"So you must be the Jackson's," she said with a definitive sales pitch in her voice. Each member of the family, along with Jeremy, stood up simultaneously as if they were called to attention by a drill sergeant.

"Hi, I'm Tiffany Brewer. I'll be talking with you today," she said cheerfully.

Mr. Jackson reached out with his hand to greet Ms. Brewer.

"Hi, Ms. Brewer, this is Brandy… and this is her boyfriend, Jeremy, who's also looking at schools."

Ms. Brewer reached for both Brandy's and Jeremy's hands. She continued to smile through the greeting process as if her smile was affixed to her face.

Ms. Brewer stepped to her left and pointed towards the offices. "Shall we?"

"Please, we'll follow you," Mr. Jackson replied. "We wouldn't have the slightest idea where to go."

"So true, so true" she replied.

Amazingly, she still held her smile. With her in the lead, the Jacksons and Jeremy walked single file through the back hall. She guided them to a room with a long wooden table and a set of chairs with deep backs and swivel wheels.

"Please, take a seat." she said with a smile.

There was a momentary silence as Ms. Brewer let everyone get situated.

Once everyone appeared to be comfortable in their chairs, Ms. Brewer looked at Brandy's parents and then Brandy.

"So I understand you're interested in attending CIU?"

"Yes ma'am. I am."

A smile appeared on Brandy's face as she responded.

Ms. Brewer nodded her head. She then looked at Jeremy.

"And what about you?"

Jeremy looked around the table.

"Yes ma'am," he replied, even though deep down he didn't know where he really wanted to go.

"What are you two interested in majoring in?" she asked.

Brandy quickly responded.

"Engineering."

Ms. Brewer looked at Jeremy.

"Umm … Clinical psychology," Jeremy replied with a little less enthusiasm than Brandy.

Ms. Brewer leaned forward in her chair and smiled.

"Well, we have a very good engineering school and our psychology department is really solid."

Jeremy grinned.

For the next hour she discussed the history of the school, dorm life, tuition, and scholarship opportunities, among other things with Brandy and Jeremy.

Brandy couldn't stop smiling and she often nodded her head. Jeremy was a little less enthusiastic. It all sounded really good, but he didn't know. This was his first school visit after all.

Finally, after nearly an hour, a tall gentleman in his mid-forties appeared. He was dressed in khakis and an orange and blue collared shirt. He knocked politely. Ms. Brewer looked back towards the door and motioned Coach Sams, the Head Baseball Coach, into the room. Coach Sams opened the door and paused momentarily as he glanced at the audience in front of him.

Ms. Brewer stood up from her chair and looked at the family.

"This is Coach Sams, the head baseball coach."

"So, which one of you is Jeremy James?" he asked playfully.

Truth be told, Coach Sams had been in communication with Coach and I for the last two years. He unsuccessfully attempted to arrange a meeting in the spring because things were just so hectic.

Jeremy sat up. Coach Sams reached for Jeremy's hand. Excited, Jeremy stumbled over his chair as he stood up.

"Nice to meet you, sir."

Coach found an empty chair across from Jeremy and sat down.

"Word has it you're thinking about attending CIU?"

"Yes sir, I am."

"Well, I've seen you play and I've talked to Coach Wilson about you. Would you like to venture out to the stadium to talk?"

Jeremy tried unsuccessfully to hide his excitement. Coach Sams looked at Mr. Jackson and then back towards Jeremy.

"Why don't you see if these wonderful people would want to join us?"

Brandy flipped her hair to her right side and nudged Jeremy gleefully.

Mr. Jackson, the sports fan he was, chimed in.

"I think I can speak for everyone here. We would love to see the facilities."

"Alright then, let's get out there." He looked at Ms. Brewer. "If you guys aren't done, I can wait outside. I didn't mean to interrupt."

"Nope. I believe we're done, unless they have more questions for me." Ms. Brewer asked.

Mr. Jackson looked to his left towards his wife and Brandy. "You guys good?"

Brandy leaned over and nudged Jeremy with her shoulder

playfully and giggled.

"I should start asking a bunch of dumb questions."

Everyone stood up, ready for their next adventure. Ms. Brewer gave Brandy and Jeremy her card.

"Don't hesitate to call or email if you have any questions, okay?"

"Well, after talking with Jeremy today, I'm sure he'll be in contact," added Coach.

A smirk crept across Jeremy's face as much as he tried to hide it. He was curious how Coach Sams knew he was visiting. Coach Sams had been eyeing Jeremy since his freshman year. Coach Wilson and I had every intention of introducing Coach Sams to Jeremy and his parents in the spring, but there never seemed to be a good time. When Coach Wilson heard Jeremy was visiting CIU with Brandy, he quickly contacted Mr. James at the bank he was the President of.

"Hey Mr. James, How are you? This is Coach Wilson."

"Oh hey Coach! How are you?"

"I'm doing well sir, thanks for asking…. The reason I'm calling is that I heard Jeremy is visiting CIU next week with Brandy."

"Yes sir, I believe he is," Mr. James responded.

"Well, the head coach, Coach Sams is very interested in Jeremy. Would you mind if I called him?"

"Coach, that would be amazing! We'd be so grateful.

We've wanted to take him to a few schools. We just didn't know where to begin."

And with that the wheels were in motion.

Jeremy walked in front of Brandy's parents. Brandy did all she could to happily keep up with him while Coach Sams walked next to Mr. Jackson.

The family followed Coach Sams' car through campus. Jeremy began to see the university differently. Brandy? Well, she was already sold.

Coach Sams' car came to a stop in front of the sports complex. In the distance sat the football field. The stadium looked much bigger up close. In front of them was the baseball stadium. Extending past the outfield was a picnic area with an umbrella in the center of each of the ten tables. Impressively, a number of the players were on the field hitting.

Everyone piled out of their respective vehicles. Proudly, Coach Sams opened his arms towards the field.

"Well, this is where the action is." With his left arm, he waved the group in his direction. "Let's go into my office where it's cooler."

Coach Sams guided them to his meeting room. Inside the room was a large wooden table, much like the one in the admissions office. On the walls were action pictures of what appeared to be past players. Coach led everyone to the table and waited for them to sit in their respective chairs before he sat in his chair.

Like the chairs back in the admission office, these were comfortable. Jeremy and Brandy couldn't get over the swiveled wheels attached to each chair. They liked them so much the wheels were a mini distraction at first. Coach Sams leaned back in his seat confidently relaxed.

"So Jeremy, what are you looking for in a school? I know you can play."

Jeremy looked to his right towards the wall. Nervous, he worked up the courage to speak.

"Well sir, I hope to play pro ball, but I want to take a different route than my brother. I want to improve my skills before going pro. I also want to experience college and earn my degree."

Coach Sams listened intently to Jeremy as Coach Sams pivoted back and forth in his chair. For the next hour Coach Sams talked to Jeremy about the college experience, the positives of attending college, and the CIU baseball program.

Coach Sams walked Jeremy and his adopted family through the baseball complex. At one point Jeremy stood silently as he watched players hit on the field.

Coach Sams nudged Jeremy with his arm.

"One thing I'm proud of is the work ethic we have instilled here at CIU. If you choose to come here, I'm sure you'll fit right in."

The day warmed up quickly. Though he didn't want to admit it, Jeremy was tired, as were the rest of the crew.

Coach Sams walked them to their car.

"Well Jeremy, I hope you decide to come here. I've had my eye on you since your freshman year."

Jeremy reached for Coaches' hand. "Thank you, sir. I'm definitely interested. I appreciate your time."

"I'll be sure to communicate what I heard with his dad and Coach Wilson," Mr. Jackson added.

"Alright, I appreciate that. Well, I hope you guys have a safe trip back to Franklin." Coach looked at Jeremy. "I look forward to hearing from you."

The Jackson family and Jeremy retreated towards their car, which sat longingly by itself while it baked in the sun. The walk seemed much longer than when they arrived. They piled into the car only to be slammed by the heat which lingered in the car.

"Geeze dad, turn on the AC. It's hot in here," Brandy bellowed dramatically in agony.

Mr. Jackson guided the car out of the parking lot while he ignored his daughter. He knew it was only a matter of time before the car would cool down.

They hadn't gone more than a mile before Brandy piped up again.

"Dad, we're hungry."

Jeremy looked at Brandy. He didn't know he was hungry.

After they stopped for a mid afternoon lunch, they headed back towards Franklin. The streets were distinctly different from Champaign. Except for the few teenagers who drove through the streets during the summer because of boredom, there was NO one on the streets. As the crew neared Brandy's house she blurted out, "I can't wait to attend CIU!"

7

Coach Jacobs

Mid August

Nearly a month had passed since Jeremy and Brandy's adventure to Central Illinois University. A number of other schools called Jeremy or Coach because they wanted Jeremy to play for their school.

For some reason, Jeremy dreaded the start of school. He rested on his bed, irritated and restless while a baseball game played on the TV.

He gathered his wallet and keys and quickly ran down the stairs towards the back door next to the kitchen.

"Mom, Dad, I'm heading over to Coach's house for a bit."

"Okay," they yelled in tandem from the living room.

"I wonder where he's going," Mr. James inquired, while he kept his face in the book he was intently reading.

Mrs. James, humored, stared at her husband for a short minute.

"Sweetie, come on. He just said he's going over to Coach Wilson's house."

"Oh, I guess I missed that."

Five minutes later Jeremy arrived at Coach Wilson's house. He slowly approached the front door. The last thing he wanted to do was bother his head Coach. When the doorbell rang, Don looked at his wife dumbfounded. It was the night before the first day of school after all.

Margaret smiled as he gruffed out loud. She stood up, straightened her pants, and walked towards the door. Out of habit, she turned on the porch light even though it was not fully dark outside. She peeked through the side window, and to her surprise Jeremy was at the door.

"Don!" she yelled, "There's someone here to see you!"

Bewildered, he yelled back. "Who is it?"

"Well, why don't you get in here and find out, you old man."

Jeremy stood quietly on the porch while he nervously waited for the door to open.

Finally, Margaret opened the door. "C'mon in," she grinned. "Coach will be with you in a moment."

Still somewhat nervous, Jeremy stepped through the doorway, worried he was interrupting something. I can totally understand why Jeremy was worried. Don had an intimidating aura about him.

Around the corner walked Don.

"Hey Jeremy, what can I do for you?"

Before Jeremy had a chance to answer, Coach motioned Jeremy to follow him.

"C'mon, let's go out back. It's beautiful out tonight."

Coach Wilson looked at his wife and smiled. "Jeremy,

would you like something to drink? Maybe an ice tea or a soda?"

Jeremy looked at Coach Wilson and then Margaret. "I'd love a soda."

In single file Coach and Jeremy walked through the kitchen and onto the back porch.

"So, what's up? What's on your mind?"

Before Jeremy had a chance to respond, Don lifted up a bowl of cherries he grabbed from the kitchen as he passed through.

"You want some cherries? They're delicious."

Jeremy didn't answer.

Don continued. "You see that tree over there? It produces the best cherries in the world, if I do say so myself."

Even though Jeremy liked cherries, he turned him down. Instead, he sat uncomfortably in his chair with his elbows resting on his knees. He tapped nervously with his right foot while he gathered his thoughts.

"Coach...what are your thoughts about CIU?"

"Why do you ask?" He scooped up a handful of cherries from the bowl.

"Well, I'm leaning towards CIU and I just wanted to get your opinion."

Coach Wilson nodded his head.

"Well, I think CIU is a great school academically and they

have a solid baseball program. Wherever you decide to go will be the right decision, because it's your decision. I know a few other schools have expressed interest in you, but it seems CIU has caught your attention over all of the others. You have to choose what you think fits you. If CIU is what fits you, then it's the best decision. You never really know until the decision has been made."

Jeremy sat and listened intently as Coach continued.

"Look at your brother. He's thriving now, but when he had to decide, there could've been a million things that could've happened, for better or for worse. Never live with regrets. Write your book, and YOUR book only."

There was silence.

Coach leaned towards Jeremy and slapped him on the knee. "Scary as crap, isn't it?"

"Yeah it is, Coach," Jeremy replied, laughing.

As the conversation drew to a close, a tired Don stood up. Jeremy hadn't finished his drink, but he received Coach's hint. He took one more quick sip and stood up as well.

Don reached out for Jeremy's hand.

"If you ever need to talk, you know where to find me. Don't forget, Coach Jacobs played in the minors as well."

After firmly shaking Coach Wilson's hand, Jeremy walked towards his car in the front of the house. Don, on the other hand, remained outside. He sat back down in his chair. He must have felt warm, because Margaret saw him holding his drink up to his forehead.

He looked up and watched several lightening bugs flutter in the light. Jeremy's car lights shrunk in size as he backed out of the driveway. Margaret peeked outside to check on her husband when she heard Jeremy's car drive away.

"You okay, sweetie?"

"Yeah, I'm just a little tired for some reason."

"Do you need to go to the doctor?"

Falling on deaf ears, he grunted. She had been married long enough to know Don was going to do what Don was going to do. Heck, I even learned that for myself while working with him through the years.

"Well, if you need anything, let me know, hun," she added sympathetically.

Don looked up at her. She could tell he was tired and didn't want to be bothered. She slid the back door shut, and Don sat quietly in his seat. Margaret peaked through the door one more time and winked at her beloved husband. He didn't notice her, because he was focused on the lightning bugs.

8

Coach Jacobs

Mid August

It was hard to believe another year of school had arrived. Jeremy woke up determined to attend CIU, major in clinical psychology, and play baseball.

Across town Brandy woke up happier than ever before. She walked through the house gleefully whistling. Downstairs her mom and dad looked at each other, befuddled.

"Why is she so happy?" her dad asked with a smirk on his face.

"I don't know. Maybe it's because she's a senior and she's excited about the future?"

"Huh, I didn't realize teenagers got excited about things like that," he replied with a straight face.

Brandy finally appeared in the kitchen.

"Morning guys!"

She sat down at the table and continued to hum happily to herself like something out of a cheerful musical. The only thing missing were song birds on her shoulder.

Her mom curiously looked at her.

"Well, aren't you in a good mood. Is everything alright?"

"Yeah, I'm excited about the year! I talked with Alexa last night. She has a way of motivating you and brightening the

46

world." She paused so she could take a breath. "I have a feeling Jeremy isn't going to go to CIU, but that's okay. If we're to be together, we'll find a way."

"Really? Well, whatever she's telling you, Alexa needs to bottle it up and sell it," Sue added.

Brandy's dad finally worked his way into the conversation.

"Did Alexa say how Julio is doing?"

Brandy rolled her eyes playfully, unsurprised by her dad's question.

"Yes, daddy she did. I guess he's doing well. Apparently, they'll be in St. Louis and Chicago a few weeks from now."

Because she lost track of time, she was surprised when Jeremy appeared at the back door.

"Oh crap, you're here," she said in a panic.

Her parents turned and noticed Jeremy at the back door. Before he had a chance to knock on the door, Rick motioned him in.

"C'mon in and join us."

Jeremy slid the door open and walked in.

"Sorry, Jer. I lost track of time. Let me run upstairs and brush my teeth."

The school parking lot was nearly empty when I pulled in. Since I started working at Franklin High School, I always parked in the same spot. Coach did as well. Strangely, he hadn't arrived even though he had often arrived before me. I think we had a little unwritten competition in that regard. The gym was extra quiet. Mike Jones, the Athletic Director, sat quietly in his office sipping on a cup of coffee he had just brewed.

"Morning, Mike. Are you ready for another school year?"

Even though I knew the answer, I figured I'd ask him anyways.

"Not really," he groaned, "But do we have a choice?" He paused, "Hey, have you talked to Coach Wilson yet today?"

"No, I haven't."

I thought it was a bit strange he hadn't appeared at school yet.

Approximately thirty minutes before school was to begin, I walked through the gym and into the main hall. The halls were slowly filling with students. Many stayed outside and listened to music on their car radios until they absolutely had to come in. I neared the stairs which led me to Coach Wilson's room.

"Coach, how are you doing?" a familiar voice asked from behind.

I turned around. Jeremy and Brandy were side by side and walking towards me. Gladly, I paused at the base of the stairs.

"Morning, guys. I hope you had a good summer?"

Both of them smiled. Brandy had an especially large grin.

I pointed upstairs.

"I was just heading upstairs to talk to Coach."

"Cool, can we go with you?" asked Jeremy.

"Yeah, we want to say good morning to him," added Brandy.

"Sure. There's nothing super important I need to see him about."

I hadn't talked to Jeremy since the beginning of the summer, so I was glad to catch up with him about his summer adventures. Brandy was one of my favorite students: motivated, a hard-worker, dedicated to school, and genuine -- which made her easy to admire. I could definitely understand why Jeremy would want to spend time with her.

To our surprise, Coach Wilson's door was locked and there was no sign he had arrived, which greatly baffled me. I peeked through the door window. "Huh," I said out loud, "I wonder where he is."

Brandy and Jeremy stood next to each other, confused.

"I'm going to the office, maybe they know something we don't. He's probably just late."

In the back of my mind though, I was becoming more worried. He didn't know what late meant after all.

The halls were filling in quickly, at least by Franklin High School standards, when I, Jeremy, and Brandy walked into the office. The secretaries were moving quicker than normal which puzzled me. I knew it was the first day, but still. I stood at the counter and wondered what was wrong. Mike came out of the principal's office visibly upset.

"Hey Mike, what's up? What's going on? Where's Coach?"

Mike stopped in his tracks and looked at me. He looked at Jeremy and Brandy and then back at me.

"Um, can you come in here, Coach?"

His voice quivered and his eyes were welled up with tears. Immediately I knew something was wrong, -- just what, I had no idea.

"Sure."

I walked around the counter. Jeremy stood on the opposite side of the counter, confused. He wasn't sure what to do.

Coach Jones led me into the principal's office. Next to the principal stood a police officer. They both looked at me somberly.

"What's wrong, guys? Is everything okay?"

Looking back, that was such a dumb question.

My boss, Mr. Simpson, couldn't make eye contact with me. Coach Jones looked out the door and then at me.

"Um, Coach… Um… Coach Wilson was found dead this morning from an apparent heart attack. Apparently, his wife went to bed early last night. When she woke up in the middle of the night, she grew worried because he wasn't in bed. He was found dead outside on the back porch.”

“Oh shit. No way!” I unintentionally said out loud.

“Yeah, man. I’m sorry. I know you guys were close.” He looked at me and then motioned with his head outside. “Do you want me to tell Jeremy or would you rather?”

“Oh hell. I’ll tell him, but believe me, I sure don’t want to.” It took all my energy not to start crying.

I stepped out of the office and looked at Jeremy. I motioned with my right hand.

“Jeremy... Brandy.”

They walked around the corner towards me.

“What’s up, Coach?” Jeremy asked. “Is everything alright? Where’s Coach Wilson?”

I paused. I couldn’t think of the right words to say. Tears had formed in my eyes. Somehow I held myself together.

It’s bad enough they both lost someone close the previous school year. Now I had to tell them they lost someone else. Yeah... that really sucked.

I took a deep breath.

“Guys, sometime last night Coach had a heart attack and he was found dead this morning.”

Jeremy stood at the door of the office. Motionless. Brandy fell to the floor like a thousand pounds were immediately put on her shoulders and she started to sob.

“Wait, what?” Jeremy asked while Brandy squeezed

Jeremy's leg and cried uncontrollably.

I paused and took another breath. I couldn't believe I had to repeat it.

"Sorry, Jeremy. Coach was found dead this morning from a heart attack."

He looked at me with tears in his eyes.

"No way, Coach... that's bullshit! I was at his house last night getting advice. No way! It must be someone else."

Jeremy quickly looked for a chair. He tried to hide his tears, but he was unsuccessful. With messed up mascara, Brandy looked at me as tears streamed down her face.

Hyperventilating she screamed, "Why?! Why?!" over and over. Hugging Jeremy with all her strength she wailed. "I'm sorry, Jeremy. I'm so sorry,"

Both, I and Coach Jones stood in the office, struggling to hide our emotions. It was tough enough one of our friends had died without the chance to say goodbye, but what really tore me up was Jeremy's obvious anguish.

He couldn't seem to catch a break.

9

Luke Fisher

Mid August

I opened my eyes as the phone buzzed the obnoxious tone Julio always had it set at. Good God, it was an awful sound, mainly because we had a late game the night before.

Finally, Julio reached across his body for his phone.

"Hello?" he said in a groggy voice.

"Wait, what happened?" I heard him ask.

Julio sat up in his bed and rested his head against the headboard. There was a long pause. From what I could tell Julio was struggling not to cry. His left hand through his hair, while his right hand clenched the phone.

Julio hung up and threw his phone to the end of the bed.

"No way... no damn way..."

"Hey man, you okay?"

I was worried about him.

He looked at me with tears in his eyes. I immediately knew something bad had happened.

"My head coach from Franklin died sometime last night."

"Dude, what?! No way! What happened?"

"Yeah, shit, no way!" he added.

Unable to speak coherently he streamed together numerous obscenities, which he rarely did.

"Hey man.. I'm sorry."

There was a pause while I tried to think of the right words. Baseball immediately came to mind.

"Are you going to be able to pitch tonight?"

It was his night in the rotation to pitch.

Instead of answering me, he sat in his bed motionless. I could see tears were running down his face. The room was uncomfortably quiet. I didn't want to bug him with questions nor did I want to make much noise, so I didn't turn on the TV. In all honesty, I didn't know what to do.

Finally, Julio looked at me.

"Dude, I'm throwing tonight. Case closed."

"Are you sure? I'm sure if you tell the coaches they'd understand."

"No! This game will be in honor of my coach. He believed in me when other people in Franklin didn't... Yeah this game will be for him."

Julio reached across the bed for his phone.

"I better call Jeremy to see how he's doing. I bet he's torn up right now. Shit, man, this fuckin sucks." he mumbled.

He sat quietly in his bed while the phone rang on the other end. Finally, Jeremy answered his phone.

"Hey Jer, how are you doing?" There was a pause. "Things are going to be okay, Jer."

He finally hung up the phone. I could tell he was in agony.

"Hey man, how's your brother?"

"Not well. He's going to be okay, he's just had a tough run this past last year. Shit, I need to call Alexa, this won't be fun."

He held the phone for several minutes until he worked up the courage to call his best friend. Much to his despair, Alexa didn't answer. I'm not surprised since it was 8:00 in the morning where we were, which meant it was 6:00 back in Palo Alto.

I looked at the clock on the table between our beds. Nearly thirty minutes had passed since Julio first received the news. Ready for a bite to eat and some coffee, I threw on some sweats and shoes. Julio, on the other hand, moved much slower. Between going for breakfast, showering, and getting dressed, the guy moved like a turtle, which was definitely not like him.

After a small breakfast down in the lobby, I made my way back up to the room. He had finally worked up the energy to shower but that was about it. By the time Julio got done, I was on my bed with a cup of coffee looking up stock quotes, which I liked to do in my spare time. After some thought, I texted Pam. I know Julio didn't tell me to do so, but I thought Pam should tell Alexa to call Julio when she had the chance. I forgot Pam liked to sleep in as opposed to Alexa who generally woke up earlier.

I wanted to ask him if he was okay but I didn't want to be a pest. After some determination, I figured if he wanted to talk he would. Neither of us really shared our feelings a whole lot. We eventually joined the rest of the team down in the lobby. Julio had a blank stare on his face the whole time. Several players made failed attempts to say hello. He would acknowledge them, but that was about it. I could tell he was in no mood to talk and so could his teammates.

As we neared the stadium, I asked him if he was alright. He ignored me. A few times his phone rang but he refused to answer.

The bus finally arrived at the stadium. When it finally came to a stop, we all filed off the bus. It was time to go to work.

The day dragged on as we prepared for our second game out of three against Milwaukee. While in the locker room, I looked at Julio a couple of different times and wondered how he was holding up. At one point, I noticed he was on his phone, slumped over with his elbows on his knees, and his phone was held up to his ear. The whole time he looked down towards the ground. Not one time did he make eye contact with any of the players as they walked by him.

I felt a tap on my shoulder. It was our manager, Carl Smith.

"Hey Coach," I said hesitantly.

You never really want the manager to tap you on your

shoulder the day of a game. The last thing you want to hear is, *"you're not playing today"* or worse yet, *"we're trading you."* So when he tapped me on my shoulder the last thing on my mind was Julio's troubles.

"So Luke, what's up with him today? Girl problems?"

"No, Coach, His high school coach died last night from a heart attack."

"Oh, damn. Why hasn't he told me?" he immediately asked as he changed his tone. "Do you think he'll be able to pitch tonight?"

"Well, he was quite adamant about starting when I asked him back in our hotel rooms."

"Huh," he paused. "Well, thanks for letting me know. I'll let him come to me then."

"Yes, Sir. No problem," I replied.

The afternoon went by rather quickly, at least for me. As game time neared, I really wanted to ask him if he was okay, but this was one time I figured questions were better left unasked.

The stadium was packed. It's amazing how full a stadium can get when a winning team is in town. Put two winning teams in the same stadium and the place really can become electric.

Since we were the away team we hit first. Sadly, our first three batters made three quick outs. It was now Julio's turn to throw. He looked as confident as ever as he sauntered towards the mound. Prior to the game, he had a certain unexplainable look in his eyes, which I had never seen before in my two years as one of his teammates. The look was kind of scary. At one point, a few of our teammates came up to me and asked if Julio was alright. I just shrugged my shoulders and refrained from going into too much detail.

From my position in centerfield, I could tell Julio was throwing the ball hard. The first inning started off well. Their first two batters struck out and the third flew out to me in centerfield. After our inability to score any runs in the second inning, we were back out on the field to play defense. Again, Julio pitched to three batters and retired all three in succession.

The next three innings had the same results for us offensively. We weren't able to get anyone across home plate even though we hit the ball hard. From atop the mound, Julio was zinging the ball across home plate. Sometimes he even reached 100 miles per hour. Many of the batters looked foolish as they swung at pitches they had no chance of hitting. I couldn't help but smile at the incredible results.

At the end of the fifth inning, I realized Julio was throwing a perfect game! I reached the bottom of the dugout steps and turned to look at the scoreboard. Yep, it was confirmed. He had given up no walks, no hits, and there were no errors. I nudged one of the guys next to me and smiled. Quietly, I motioned with my head towards the scoreboard. Lesson number one in baseball, NEVER acknowledge a perfect game or a no hitter to the pitcher involved. Talk about a MAJOR jinx!

It didn't help that we hadn't scored a run either. The sixth inning came and went because Julio was able to get the next three batters out.

Seven innings had come and gone and neither team had scored a run. This was a full on pitcher's duel with Julio in the middle of a perfect game. You could've cut the intensity with a knife.

I was the first to hit in the top of the eighth. I approached home plate and glanced towards the third base coach who did his typical clapping and cheering. I looked into the dugout and noticed Julio off in the corner by himself. The last thing I wanted to do was let him down.

I took a deep breath then stepped up to hit. The pitcher, Frank Johnson -- a reliever for Milwaukee -- looked like Paul Bunyan on top of the mound. Since this was his first inning of action, he was throwing the ball hard. Hell, when the ball crossed home plate, I could hear it buzzing. Shit!

Two pitches had been thrown: one ball and one strike. Prior to the third pitch, I took a deep breath. The noise around me somehow disappeared and everything moved in slow motion as the next 100 miles per hour pitch crept towards me. My eyes widened like saucers. I swung at the ball and made contact like nothing I had felt before. It felt awesome!

The ball bounced off my bat towards left field. I couldn't help but watch as it drifted over the outfield wall. I ran around the bases laughing uncontrollably. I must have looked like a big dork. As I passed third base, I pointed at Julio.

"That's for you!" I exclaimed.

Of course he smiled, but that was it.

Unable to score any more runs, we sprinted onto the field. We had two more innings to keep them off the scoreboard.

I watched Julio warm up. In between pitches I would glance at the scoreboard. Holy. Crap. The dude was still pumping the ball past home plate at speeds over 100 miles per hour. I looked at my teammate in right field and then my teammate in left. We all smiled at each other.

The first batter struck out on three pitches. I glanced towards my teammate in left field. We both laughed at how bad the batter looked. Julio still had total command of the strike zone. I honestly feared as the game went deeper that I would get lazy and a ball would be hit in between me and one of my teammates in the outfield.

There were just five more outs to go!

The next batter up watched the first pitch go by for a strike. The next pitch was thrown right down the middle of the plate and SMACK! The ball was lined towards third base. The third basement didn't even have to move. it was hit right at him.

Yep, sometimes it's better to be lucky than good. I hid my face behind my glove while I laughed nervously.

There were now just four more outs to go!

Julio stepped on top of the mound to face the next batter. The first two pitches zipped home and hit the outside part of the plate for ball one and ball two. The last thing he wanted to do was fall behind in the count. He didn't want to give the batter anything to hit. He definitely didn't want to walk the batter either. The next two pitches were thrown for strikes, which evened the count to two balls and two strikes. All he needed was one more pitch. Julio went into his windup and threw the ball down the middle of the plate.

CRACK!

The ball bounced off the bat and streaked deep into left center. Both I and the left fielder frantically sprinted towards the wall. Finally, not more than five feet from the wall, I lepted into the air and caught it as I banged into the wall. It hurt like hell but I didn't care because it was the third out and the perfect game was still intact! Yowsa, that was close!

I was so excited that I ran from the outfield towards the dugout in a full sprint. Julio came up and nudged me while wearing a huge cheesy grin on his face.

"Nice catch dude!"

He stood next to me for a few seconds with a smile

painted on his face, obviously at peace with the world.

"Hey, Julio! Mow the next three down," I said confidently, even though I knew I had just broken baseball code 101. Never hint to the pitcher he was in the middle of a perfect game or a no hitter.

Julio looked at me and smiled. "That's what I intend to do."

Our team was unable to score any more runs, so I gathered my glove and ran towards centerfield. Once I reached my position, I turned around and noticed Julio on the pitching mound. From my vantage point he seemed as relaxed as ever. In the back of my mind, I hoped I didn't jinx him. That was all but answered when the first two batters of the inning sat down after making quick outs.

The fans stood on their feet in hopes of being a part of history at the expense of their own team. Torn, the fans cheered in between pitches for Julio, but cheered for their batter who may or may not ruin the perfect game.

Julio was quickly ahead in the count. The count was no balls and two strikes. He stood on top of the mound and paused for a moment before he went into his windup. The next pitch was up and in, but for some reason the batter swung at the pitch.

"Strike three!"

Julio just threw a perfect game!

He fell to his knees and threw his hands into the air. In jubilation, the rest of the team ran to the mound to celebrate. Nevermind I wound up hitting the game winning homerun, but I didn't care. I was excited for him.

Inside the dugout, Manager Smith sat and waited patiently for Julio. After the team celebrated on the field, Julio walked towards the dugout.

"Julio, get your butt over here." There was a pause. "I understand you lost your former Coach last night?"

Somewhat surprised, Julio didn't respond right away. "Yes sir, I did."

"Well I don't know how you did it today, but it was nothing less than a work of art. I still have to talk to management, but I'm sure they'll approve. I want you to take the next few days off. Go home and be with your family and friends."

A tear formed in the corner of Julio's eye.

The locker room was bustling with excitement. Not only did we win a big game, but our guy threw a perfect game. As excited as I was, I knew the driving force for the perfect game was Julio's suffering which saddened me. Across the way, I watched Julio pretend to be excited. He hid his emotions from the rest of the team, but I knew better. From time to time Julio would look at me, flash a small smile, and then look away.

Finally, after I showered and cleaned up, I walked over to

Julio's locker. "Hey man, can I sit down?"

Julio looked up at me with tears in his eyes. "Yeah... man... feel free..." he stammered.

"Are you going to be okay?" I asked.

I wanted him to know I was there for him.

Julio forced out a smile. "Yeah, it's been a tiring night. By the way, great hit tonight. You do know you won the game, right?"

That was just like Julio. He always found a way to pass the credit on to others less deserving.

"Well, let's get out of here. It's been a long night." I nudged him in the side.

As we stood up his cell phone rang.

"Shit. It's Alexa."

10

Coach Jacobs
Mid August

Even though Alexa got the earliest possible flight home, she wasn't able to arrive in St. Louis until early afternoon. Julio was able to get an early flight into St. Louis, so he waited patiently at the airport for her arrival. With her shoulders slumped and a heavy heart, she walked through the airport towards the main terminal. Finally, Julio appeared. Try as she did, she couldn't hide her tear filled eyes. She dropped her bags to her feet as if they were full of weights. Julio stood in front of her tired and saddened. Her lips quivered with despair as she opened her arms for a needed hug. Glad to see his best friend, Julio engulfed her into his arms.

"I wish I was at the game last night," she whispered.

"I wish you were too."

Alexa squeezed Julio as tight as she could. Overwhelmed with emotion, she began to cry as she sunk her face into his chest.

They stood in the middle of the terminal lost in emotion without much care for the people around them.

"Why? why?" she cried.

Alexa pulled herself away from Julio. Her hands continued to grasp onto Julio's arms while her manicured nails lightly dug into his skin.

She looked up at him as tears dripped from her cheeks.

"Nothing better happen to you."

Julio pulled her towards him and held her against his body.

"Don't worry, I'll always be here for you," he whispered.

She squeezed him tighter.

"That's BS. Don't tell me that. You have no way of knowing."

"You know what I mean."

"I know, I'm just tired of losing good people in my life."

After Julio gathered Alexa's bags, they quietly walked out of the airport, hand in hand, towards the parking garage where their car was waiting for them. During much of the drive home small talk was absent. Small talk seemed like a waste of energy.

Finally the two arrived in Franklin later that afternoon. The town was eerily quiet.

"Don't take me home yet," she said with a saddened face.

"Where'd you like to go?"

"Your place. I want to see Jeremy."

In between sniffles, Alexa half-heartedly laughed.

"You know, in my two years of knowing you in this town, we never hung out at your place."

"That's because your place was the place to be!"

Playfully, Alexa slapped Julio on the arm.

"Oh, shut up."

"Well it certainly wasn't my place. God forbid you or anyone else was seen at my house... or have you forgotten," he asked as he glanced in Alexa's direction.

"Wow, I hadn't forgotten, but it's amazing how at the time it was so..." She stopped in mid sentence. She was unable to complete her thoughts.

"Yeah, I'm ready for my brother to get out of this town." He paused. "Though I have to say, it's been cool to see Jeremy grow up here."

Alexa began to respond when her eyes widened with excitement. To their surprise, Jeremy, Brandy, Cali, and a few of the other baseball players were in lawn chairs next to Julio's garage. Alexa yelled with joy as she frantically attempted to open the front door of the car as it came to a stop. She repeatedly pulled on the door handle. Finally, the door flung open. Alexa jumped out of the vehicle and ran towards Jeremy. Jeremy didn't recognize the car -- it was a rental after all -- but when he saw Alexa he leapt to his feet. Brandy's face widened, excited to see Alexa as well.

Though Cali was just a junior, she recognized Julio. She and her dad attended some of the games while she was in eighth grade. Though her main love was golf, her parents were friends of Don's so she knew about Julio and Jeremy when they first arrived in Franklin. She grinned widely, excited to finally have the chance to meet the pitcher she grew up hearing so much about and watched from the bleachers.

Jeremy ran up to Alexa.

"Here's my future sister-in-law," he said jokingly.

Jeremy stepped back. Julio was on the other side of the car.

"Well look who's here everyone, Mr. Perfect Game."

Julio, shrugged his shoulders and grinned.

Alexa captured the attention of the other guys. Of course, she was totally oblivious and didn't concern herself with them. Cali on the other hand punched Josh, a former teammate of Julio's in the arm.

"Geeze Josh, can you not stare?"

Josh quickly looked away.

Julio walked into the garage and pulled out two more lawn chairs. For close to an hour Julio told the awe inspired ones around him about his perfect game and life in the major leagues. Alexa, Brandy, and Cali got distracted a few times as Alexa shared stories about Stanford with them.

11

Coach Jacobs
Mid August

I wish it was just a bad dream, but it wasn't. Even though my job as a P.E. teacher was rather easy, the day I found out Coach Wilson had died was one of the toughest days in my life. The next morning I sat in the kitchen and contemplated skipping work while I sipped my coffee and ate my toast. Heck, my wife even urged me to call in sick, but I felt a need to be at school for the kids.

Somberly, I walked into the school building. The halls seemed emptier than normal. I chalked it up to missing my friend already. I wanted to cry and I did in my office where it was quiet and private. It was tough.

I sat in my office and thought about the many long nights I had with Coach talking about baseball. I don't know how our wives put up with us, but they did. It's probably because they knew the importance of our friendship and our love for baseball. Whenever we sat on his back porch he would inevitably offer me a bowl of cherries or a glass of cherry lemonade, which made me smile everytime.

I turned around when I heard a shuffling of feet. To my surprise, Brandy was at my office door.

"Coach - um - are you free to talk?" she asked hesitantly.

I set the folders I had in my hand down. In retrospect, I couldn't tell you what were in those stupid folders. I think I was just trying to look busy.

"Sure. C'mon in."

Brandy walked into the office, but remained standing. She rocked back and forth from her left to her right foot. I could sense she was uncomfortable.

"What's on your mind?"

"Um -- Could I ask a favor from you?"

She refrained from making eye contact with me.

"Yeah, what's up?"

"Well Coach, can you keep an eye on Jeremy? Follow up with the college coaches and I don't know..."

I sat up and smiled. "No worries. I will do all I can to make sure he makes it through the year… how are you though?"

Brandy opened her mouth but paused before she spoke. "I'm well considering the circumstances, I guess."

She finally sat in the chair in front of my desk. She settled her arms onto the arm rests and looked at me, looked away, then looked back at me again. I couldn't tell if she wanted to say anything more, so I quietly waited.

She quietly sat in her chair for what must have been five minutes. She didn't even say one word to me. Her eyes were red, probably from crying. I waited patiently, even if that meant we sat in our seats, speechless.

"Thanks coach for your time. I appreciate it," she said quietly.

Brandy stood up, paused, and weakly smiled.

"Hey Brandy."

She turned and looked at me.

"Hang in there. That's what Coach would want."

Brandy took a deep breath as her lips began to quiver. She turned towards the door and quietly left the room. The room was quiet again.

The end of the day finally arrived. I thought it would never come. I looked towards the gym door when I heard it slam shut. It was the principal, Mr. Simpson.

"Coach, can I have a word with you?"

I turned towards him. "Sure, what's up?"

"Well, I've been talking to some of the school board members, and well, with the circumstances the way they are, would you be interested in being the head coach this upcoming year?" He paused for a moment. "I can't think of a better person to be the head coach."

I didn't know whether to feel flattered or guilty.

"Can we talk later? I was hoping to get home early. It's been a long day."

Mr. Simpson reached out with his hand to conclude the conversation.

"Sure, coach. We'll talk later."

The next day was Don's wake. Like the previous day, the last place I wanted to be was at work. Thankfully, the day didn't drag on too much. Once the final bell rang, I gathered my things and drove across town.

At the funeral home, many of the players, co-workers, and friends sat in silence throughout the room. Like two peas in a pod, Julio and Jeremy sat next to each other. Jeremy's eyes were filled with tears. At times, Brandy would lay her head on Jeremy's shoulder.

After Julio left the wake, he went for a run. When he returned from his run, he and Jeremy drove up to the ballfield. It had been a long time since the two had thrown the ball to each other.

Like the good ole days, the two whirled the ball back and forth without a single spoken word. As they continued to throw, the weight on Jeremy's shoulders from the past few days melted away and a smile crept across his face.

"Hey bro," Jeremy yelled, "When are you going to bust the move and ask Alexa to marry you?"

Julio laughed.

"Don't know, I haven't really thought about it. I mean, she's only in her second year at Stanford and I just broke into the majors." He paused. "Why do you ask?"

"Don't know. I guess I'm just curious."

"Trust me… You will be one of the first ones I'll tell,

okay? I promise... Alexa didn't put you up to this did she?"

Jeremy smiled.

"Nope."

The two bantered back and forth until they no longer could throw anymore because of the dark sky. The orange glow had finally disappeared over the horizon.

As they neared the car, Julio put his right arm around his brother.

"I look forward to the day I'm mowing you down in the majors."

"You think I'm good enough?"

Julio looked at him in disbelief. "Please!"

There was a momentary silence.

"Let's get home. I need to pack for Houston and I'm sure mom has dinner ready."

Jeremy had no desire to see his brother leave, but he knew Julio had a job to do.

Julio and Jeremy sat up and talked baseball late into the night. Neither one of them were night owls, but because of his job, Julio had become accustomed to late nights.

Julio finally turned off their bedroom light. The neighborhood was quiet, which was typical for a weeknight in Franklin. Across town, Alexa sat quietly on her porch talking to her mom about college while she sipped her coffee. Several streets down, Brandy sat out on her back porch with Cali and contemplated the year ahead. Lonely, Brandy wished Jeremy was next to her.

Eventually like the rest of the town, Alexa and Brandy somberly went to bed in their respective houses.

12

Coach Jacobs
Mid August

Julio rolled over as his alarm buzzed repeatedly. Jeremy covered his head with a pillow, hoping Julio would turn off the alarm. Julio eventually reached over and hit the snooze button, which temporarily stopped the insanity. Everything went back to normal... until the alarm began buzzing again seven minutes later.

"Turn that thing off!" Jeremy bellowed in agony after seven minutes of silence.

Unconcerned for Jeremy's wishes, Julio slowly turned on his side and pressed the off button on the alarm.

Jeremy rolled over on his bed.

"Man, what time is it?"

"It's 5:30...Well, back to work," Julio mumbled.

Julio slowly walked towards the bathroom. Jeremy continued to lay motionless in his bed like a slug. He had little desire to get out of bed and go to school.

Julio cleaned himself off and slowly walked down the stairs towards the kitchen for a cup of coffee and a bagel. Not long after he arrived in the kitchen, his dad appeared.

Mr. James walked in and poured himself a cup of coffee. He smiled when he noticed his eldest son take a sip of coffee.

"Since when did you start drinking coffee?"

Julio was sure his dad had seen him drink coffee before. Julio sat back in his chair and pondered his dad's question.

"I think I started drinking coffee when I was in Utah last year."

His dad laughed.

"Well, I was sure you weren't drinking coffee while you were here. I figured Alexa would get you on it at some point."

"So dad, how's Jeremy doing?"

"Oh, I don't know. Some days he's depressed and lost, while other days he's pretty darn good. I know Brandy has been good for him."

A few minutes passed when Julio, in between sips, looked at his dad.

"You know, I hated it when we moved here. At the time this move really sucked. But in retrospect, I have to say, things turned out alright."

Mr. James nodded his head. "Well, good. I'm glad you feel that way." Mr. James paused. "I know it was tough on the two of you at first, but you definitely came into your own."

Julio lifted his cup of coffee into the air.

"And, if we didn't move here, I wouldn't have met Alexa."

"Cheers to that, son." his dad replied with a smile.

Julio lowered his cup of coffee.

"It's crazy how things turn out in life."

There was another pause in the conversation. By now Julio's mom had made her way into the kitchen.

"What are my favorite men talking about?" She asked with an awfully perky smile for such an early time of the day.

"Well hun, our son just admitted the move here was a good one," Mr. James said while he continued to sip his coffee.

"Oh he did, did he?" she replied confidently. "It's about time one of these boys admits it."

Julio raised his coffee cup.

"Cheers to that, mom."

The conversation drifted from one topic to another until Julio looked at the wall clock. As much as he hated to, he knew he had to leave. Julio had a plane to catch and a team to join. He ran upstairs to gather his bags and say goodbye one last time to his brother.

Jeremy, not ready to see his brother leave, embraced him.

"Hang in there, bro," Julio whispered. "This year is going to be a good year for you."

"Thanks, man."

Julio turned away as if he was going to leave. He paused and looked back at his brother.

"Keep your head up. Don't let this all bring you down. This is your senior year. Embrace it."

There was silence.

"I mean it. Keep your head up."

Jeremy hugged his brother one last time.

Julio walked out of the bedroom and down the stairs. He gave each of his parents one more farewell hug. As painful as it was for him to leave, he knew he had to get back to work.

In an attempt to switch gears, Julio tried to think about his job, but with very little luck.

13

Pam Thomson

Mid September

It was late afternoon when Alexa straggled into the apartment. After fumbling with her bag and keys, she plopped down on the couch. I looked at her and smiled.

As for myself, I was in the middle of graphing some supply and demand curves or some boring shit like that. I was, afterall, an economics major. Don't get me wrong. I love economics, but just not what I was doing at the time.

It's hard to believe it had been barely a year since I first met Alexa. We were roommates our freshman year at Stanford and, as it so happened, I started to date Luke, Julio's friend and teammate. Yeah, he caught my eye the first time I saw him at a minor league game. We were there to watch Julio and I saw Luke in the distance.

I always admired Alexa. I wouldn't exactly say I was jealous of her because I was just as smart and equally hard working. There was a pure quality about her. It was hard not to like her and she seemed to like everyone. It was kind of sickening at times.

I looked at Alexa and smiled.

"How were your classes today, gorgeous?"

"Uggg. They sucked," she groaned as she dramatically

threw her head onto the back of the couch.

Alexa did have a flare for the dramatic, but I loved her just the same. Well, most of the time anyways.

She lifted her head up and looked at me.

"So how was your day?"

I paused because I had to actually think about what I did that day.

"Well, outside of my homework it hasn't been a bad one."

I put down my work and turned towards Alexa.

"You look tired. You want some coffee?"

Alexa ran her hand through her hair and ruffled it up while her legs were folded up underneath her.

She smiled.

"I would love a cup... Pam, you're the best."

I walked into the kitchen and looked for one of her favorite mugs. It's funny how the smallest things can make someone smile. After a minute or two, I was back in the living room.

When I reappeared, Alexa's heels were off her feet and lying on the floor. Don't get me wrong, I loved to wear heels, but I don't know how she did it every freakin' day. She had some tough feet I guess. Then again, she did look pretty damn hot in them.

A smile raced across her face as she reached for her cup of coffee.

"Thank you sooo much. You're the best!"

I went into the kitchen and came back with a cup of coffee for myself. It was a good time for a study break, so I sat down on the opposite end of the couch. Neither one of us were very big, so there was plenty of room on the couch for the both of us.

She took a sip.

"Ohh, now THAT'S delicious." She paused. "What's Luke doing this off season?"

"I don't know. We hadn't really talked about it, but I think he's staying in San Fran."

She took another sip of her beloved coffee.

"Yeah, Julio is as well. At least, I think he is. We haven't talked about it much either."

We both giggled.

"Geeze, Alexa. Do we even talk to our men?"

Alexa smiled.

"God, Pam. Have you tried talking to Julio?"

"Yes, I have. That's why I'm asking you."

I paused to take a refreshing sip of my coffee.

"God, Alexa. What are we doing with these guys?"

Alexa playfully slapped me on my leg.

"Oh shut up. You know you're into Luke. Don't even tell me you're not."

I innocently smiled.

"Yeah, you're right...you're right."

"It's wild to think they only have a few more weeks to go." I added. "Well, I guess I need to get back to studying...shit."

"Yeah...thanks for the coffee. You know Luke is lucky to have you. I have a feeling that guy was such a player in college."

She paused and grinned as she continued to look at me.

"You have just enough edge to keep that boy in line. I mean, look at you. You have that long brunette hair and your tattoos." Alexa then playfully winked. "Yeah, he's one lucky guy."

I stood up, stretched myself out and smiled.

"Thanks. I'll take that as a compliment."

Several minutes passed. Alexa hadn't moved. She continued to quietly sip her coffee while she fiddled with her phone.

"Alexa?"

"Yes?"

"How's Julio's brother doing? He had a rough patch for a while, didn't he?"

Alexa looked up from her phone and stared at me.

She took a deep breath.

"Yeah his coach died a little over a month ago. He was Julio's coach as well."

"Ahhh, so how's he doing?"

Alexa again laid her head on the back of the couch.

"Yeah... he seems to be doing okay. It's been kind of weird but he's been dating his friend, Brandy, since this summer."

"Why would you say it's been weird?"

Alexa lifted her head off the couch.

"Don't you remember? His former girlfriend killed herself last spring."

"Ahh yeah… I do remember that."

"Yeah, well, most times I would have said it was too quick to be dating someone else, but those two were friends before Jamie's death and I think they just naturally started dating. It wasn't anything forced."

"Well, it's a good thing they have a friend like you."

Alexa didn't respond. I'm not so sure she knew what to say. Sometimes compliments are the toughest things to reply to.

14

Coach Jacobs

Early October

It was a quiet Friday morning before school. Jeremy approached my office door. I was pretending to be busy as I shuffled through papers, went through folders, and cleaned out the file cabinets. Looking back, I seemed to do that a lot. Sometimes I wonder if I actually did any teaching. Then again, I was a P.E. teacher.

"You busy, Coach?" he asked shyly while standing in the middle of the doorway.

"Nah... come on in, bud. What's up?"

Morning conversations with Jeremy were nothing new. He found his normal seat directly in front of my desk.

"Well Coach, I am going to visit CIU tomorrow and I want your opinion."

"What do your parents think?"

"They think I should wait to see where I get drafted, assuming I get drafted."

Amused, I replied. "You don't think you'll get drafted?"

"C'mon, Coach. I didn't have the best season last year."

"No... no. You didn't. But, at the same time, I think your season was better than you give yourself credit."

Jeremy sat back in his chair.

"My goal is to get us back to Springfield."

"You wanna get back to Springfield, huh?"

Jeremy sat up in his seat.

"Yes, sir. I've been talking to some of the guys and we're so ready for the season to begin. I know Kory is especially ready. He's been working his butt off to get stronger."

He paused.

"Do you think we'll have a good enough team?"

I paused for a second. I didn't want to say the wrong thing.

"I don't think our team will be as deep as the one that won state, but our pitching will be better," he said with a small grin. At that moment, the school bell rang.

Jeremy lifted himself up from the chair.

"You feeling better?"

"Yes, sir. I am," he said as he reached out to shake my hand. "Thanks for your time. I'll let you know my decision over the weekend."

The next morning, Jeremy rolled over in his bed when his alarm began to buzz loudly. He sat up and rubbed his eyes. The soft orange glow from the sunrise began to work through his window. He glanced out the window and grinned.

He sat back down on his bed and looked at his phone. It wasn't uncommon for Brandy to send a late night text message. To his disappointment, there weren't any messages. He stretched himself out on his bed and contemplated the long day ahead.

After several lazy minutes, he sauntered into the bathroom to shower and prepare for the day. As soon as he stepped out of the shower, he looked at the time. He quickly panicked. Brandy would arrive at any moment. As opposed to their last visit, Brandy would be going with Jeremy and his parents to CIU to visit the campus for the day. He had a good feeling about CIU, but he wanted to visit the school one more time. It was, after all, a big decision and he wanted to make the right one.

Like most Saturday nights, I was comfortably sitting on the couch in the living room with the lights off and the television blaring. One of the major college football games of the week was on. Enamored in the game, I ignored everything around me, not intentionally of course. At one point my wife called for me, but I had no clue what she said. Though, I'd never tell her that piece of information. I felt my phone vibrate and to my surprise it was a text from Jeremy.

I'm definitely going to CIU

Minutes later he sent me another text.

Let's go to state in honor of Coach

I smiled.

15

Luke Fisher

Early October

After Julio's perfect game, I surely thought we'd stay in first place. Despite my wishes, the team fell apart. Julio pitched a number of solid games, but he still came up on the losing end. Our offense, though -- I swear, we couldn't hit our way out of a paper sack, we were so bad. All in all, the last month of the season really sucked! The last day of the regular season finally arrived and we had no hope of reaching the playoffs.

Luckily for Julio, he didn't have to pitch in the last game. I mean, who in the world would want to pitch in the last game of the season knowing the season was over after the game. I, on the other hand, was in the starting lineup and playing centerfield.

"Julio!" I yelled out as I approached his locker.

"Luke! What's going on?"

His smile lifted my spirits.

"How are you doing?"

"Yeah, I'm just tired. This has been a long year."

I couldn't have agreed more.

"How about going out for a drink after the game this evening?"

I paused after I remembered he was just twenty.

"In your case, a soda."

He leaned up against his locker.

"Yeah man, we haven't in awhile. Just you and I, not the girls?"

"Yep, just you and I."

He smiled.

Later that afternoon, we finally went out onto the field one last time for the season. The stadium was half full, or in our eyes, half empty -- if even that. Julio sat in the dugout relaxed like I'd never seen him before. All he needed were some shades, a recliner, and a glass of cold lemonade and he would've been set for the day. Before long, the game was in the seventh inning and then the eighth inning. The game finally ended and we won. Kind of anti-climatic in retrospect.

Once the game ended, the players migrated into the clubhouse. It may have been the fastest exit I had ever seen. I guess everyone was ready to be done, since we weren't in the playoffs. I looked over and noticed Julio was nearly dressed. He must have gotten lessons from SuperMan because he was quick!

He looked at me and smiled. With his hands he motioned me to hurry. Moments later he was on his phone. I never asked, but chances are he was talking to Alexa.

As I was tying my shoes, another pair of shoes crept into my line of site. I looked up. Humored, I started to laugh.

"Julio, are you in a hurry or something? Geeze!"

"C'mon, man. You're so slooow."

After I tied my shoes, I stood up.

"Do we want to take our bags?"

"Nah, let's get them later in the week."

He was obviously ready to leave.

Julio and I opened our respective car doors and plopped down in the seats as if we hadn't sat for a year. Thankfully, Julio had driven us to the stadium.

"Dude, is it me or are you tired?"

"No, it's definitely not you."

"Man, what a year this has been."

He paused as he glanced silently ahead. After a deep breath he looked at me.

"Damn, this was a crazy year."

It was definitely an emotional year for Julio.

"Where to, my friend?" He asked after he started the ignition.

"What about pizza?"

Though he didn't mention the place specifically, I knew exactly where he was referring to and I got quite excited. It's kind of sad. We were turning into two old men.

Julio enthusiastically slammed his right hand against the steering wheel.

"Great! Let's get some pizza then!"

Humored, I shook my head.

"Alright then, let's get our butts out of here!" as I threw my hands emphatically into the air.

We sat motionless in the car when he pulled into the parking lot. To a stranger, we probably looked like trouble.

Finally, we walked into the joint for a few slices of pizza and a cold beverage. After we sat in our seats, Julio nervously looked around as if he was stalking the place out.

"You okay, man?"

Julio leaned back and stretched his arms above his head.

"Yeah, just tired."

After a minute or two, the waitress finally appeared and took our drink orders. He ordered his standard soda while I ordered a beer, something I didn't do very often -- especially during the season. When the drinks finally arrived, Julio held his soda into the air and smiled.

"To our first year!"

I held my drink in the air and tapped his glass.

"To our first year!" I repeated.

Eventually, the restaurant thinned out.

I noticed Julio stare down at the table.

"What's up? You okay?" I asked.

He glanced up at me and then he looked back down towards the straw wrapper he was fidgeting with.

"Why...why do you ask?"

"Well, I've known you for two years now and in those two years I have learned your little expressions. So, what's up?"

"A lot's on my mind I guess, with Alexa and all."

"Dude, wait, what?" I asked surprisingly. "What's going on with you and Alexa?"

"I just don't know what she's thinking. I love her, but I'm not ready for anything like marriage and I'm afraid she is."

I sat back in my chair and took a sip of my beer.

"So... wait. She hasn't alluded to marriage yet and you're worried she's wanting to get married?" I asked sarcastically. "Dude, you two have a good thing going. She's in school some forty minutes from you with two years left. Unless she brings it up, keep doing what you're doing."

The last thing I wanted to do was give him too much advice. He had to live his own life.

"So, how's your brother doing?"

I kind of wanted to change the subject.

"I don't know. I haven't talked to him lately. I believe he's leaning towards college."

"Oh yeah, where abouts?"

"I believe he's looking at Central Illinois University," he stated in between pizza bites.

The conversation continued for the next thirty minutes while we enjoyed our pizza and drinks. Eventually, we were the only two patrons in the place. We were actually fine with that and so was the waitress. Maybe because we were low maintenance or maybe because we were professional players and she hoped for a nice tip. Either way, it worked for me.

Julio looked at his phone and noticed the time.

"Shoot man, it's nearly 10pm. We need to get out of here."

"Why?" I asked curiously. "It's not like we have to get up tomorrow morning for any games."

"Good point," Julio responded humorously.

He took a sip of his drink then leaned back in his chair. I could tell he was tired.

After we paid the bill, Julio looked at me.

"Hey, let's make next year a year to talk about."

"That's a deal."

I hoped we made enough of a splash to return next year. Nothing could be taken for granted. After the finish our team had, we knew everyone on the team was expendable -- including us.

16

Luke Fisher

Mid October

Unlike the previous off season, I decided to stay in San Francisco and train with Julio. Of course, Julio couldn't pass up the chance to tease me. Though he wasn't totally wrong, Julio was under the impression I stayed in the area because of Pam. Needless to say, he had to constantly remind me of that. My mom wanted me to come home for the winter, but I figured if my parents and sister wanted to see me bad enough they'd fly out to San Francisco to visit.

It's hard to believe Pam and I had only known each other for a few months. I'll never forget the day I first saw her. Julio and I were in San Jose for our minor league debut. Pam was actually there with Alexa to cheer Julio on. Yeah, when I saw her something told me I would be dating that girl. To this day, I still can't believe she was an economics major!

Except for a few dedicated people, the gym was pretty quiet, probably because it was morning. Julio looked at his shorts with a surprised look on his face.

He muttered a few incoherent words as he pulled his phone out of his pocket.

A smile flashed across his face.

"Well, I guess my brother has decided to attend college."

"Oh yeah? Where?"

"Looks like he's going to CIU."

"Yeah, I remember you mentioning that to me before. It's a good baseball school."

We went back to our workout. A few minutes later Julio nudged me.

"If Jeremy came to visit, could you talk to him about what to expect in college?"

I smiled.

"Sure. I'd be happy to. I can always talk to him on the phone. You don't have to fly him out here."

"Yeah I know, but I'm sure he'd like the trip."

Finally, after several weeks, Julio and I stood at the terminal awaiting Jeremy's arrival into San Francisco.

Even though Julio had seen Jeremy in August, I could tell he was quite excited. Equally excited was Alexa who decided to skip class to greet him as well. As for me, I had nothing else better to do.

Like a herd of buffalo, a large group of people flowed from the terminal. Both Julio and Alexa anxiously worked to spot Jeremy.

Repeatedly Alexa asked, "Do you see him?" Which of course humored me.

"Finally!" Alexa shrieked with excitement. She frantically tugged on Julio's arm.

"There he is! There he is!"

Jeremy and Julio smiled when they made eye contact. Alexa ran up to Jeremy and nearly tackled the poor guy. She was so thrilled to see him.

As for me, I stayed back and watched. It was obvious those two guys cared for each other. I could also tell Alexa loved Jeremy like her long lost brother.

We piled into Julio's car after winding our way through the parking lot. For some reason, airport parking lots are especially confusing.

"You hungry, Jer?" asked Julio.

Jeremy was in the front seat next to his brother who was driving. I sat next to Alexa in the back. She was still evidently excited to see Jeremy. She usually had a smile on her face, but this was too damn much. As for me, I sat back and grinned as I watched them interact. I was kind of jealous of the three.

A few minutes down the road Alexa tapped Jeremy on the shoulder.

"You like pizza?"

Jeremy shook his head.

"I never turn down pizza."

Julio looked at him and then me through the mirror.

"You're paying right, Jer? Luke, didn't he say he was buying us dinner?"

"Yeah, I think you said something about that," I added.

Alexa slapped me on the leg.

"Jer, ignore these guys. They're just being mean. They can afford to buy us pizza."

"Buy 'us'? Since when did it become 'us'?" Julio jokingly asked.

"That doesn't even deserve a response," she responded in a huff.

It's amazing how a little fun banter can make the time fly. Before I knew it, we were in the parking lot of *Ricky's Pizza*. It didn't take long for us to pile out of the car, walk into the restaurant, and sit down in a booth.

"I understand you're wanting to play college ball?" I asked from across the table.

Jeremy shook his head.

"Yeah, I wasn't sure until I visited CIU. I fell in love with their campus."

"That's so cool!" Alexa added.

"Well, speaking from experience, it's a lot of work juggling ball and school, but it's a great experience."

Jeremy took a sip of his water.

"Did you come out of school a better player?"

"Oh, without a doubt." I paused. "The thing is... you have to do what's best for you. For example, I could've gotten injured any of my four years while at Florida. Or take your brother, he could've gotten injured one of the last two years.

It's a crapshoot no matter what. That's why I say you have to do what's best for you. Also, no one can take away your degree if you go to college."

A silence fell upon the table.

"What's your major going to be?" Alexa asked.

A grin ran across his face which led me to believe he was making the right decision.

"Psychology."

"Oh wow!" she added.

Julio grinned.

I wanted to ask him why psychology, but I didn't want to be nosey.

Finally, our pizza arrived. You would've thought we hadn't eaten in days. Thankfully, Alexa only had a few small slices.

As we devoured the pizza, Jeremy looked at Julio.

"How many pieces have you had?"

Julio smiled with amusement.

"Go ahead and take the last piece, Jer. I don't need it."

Jeremy looked at me. I could tell he wanted the last piece. The last thing I was going to do was stand in the middle of him and the final slice. There was really only one option.

"Take it."

After we paid for the pizza, we rolled ourselves out of the booth and walked slowly towards the car. An orangish glow appeared in the distance as the sun slowly dropped below the horizon. It was quite beautiful.

The drive back to the apartment was a quiet one. Though it wasn't very late, Jeremy was probably tired. The time change can really do a number on someone. In all actuality, outside of the long hot days during the summer, the change in time zones was one of the biggest challenges when traveling throughout the baseball season.

Sunday morning rolled around. For some reason, I was up prior to Julio's and Jeremy's exodus to the airport. Jeremy sat down in the chair across from me as I sipped my coffee.

"Thanks for your input this weekend. It was appreciated."

"No problem, bud. I don't know if I helped any but I definitely can speak from experience. At the end of the day, you have to do what's best for you and no one else. I personally feel you're making a good decision. You'll love college."

Jeremy reached towards me with his hand.

"Thanks so much," he said with a smile.

Julio came around the corner.

"You ready to go, Jer?"

Jeremy picked his bag up off the floor. He walked towards the door and stopped to look at me.

"Thanks again and good luck next year!"

Julio opened the apartment door. Both of them filed out one by one. After Julio closed the door, it became quiet again.

17

Pam Thomson

Mid January

Well, the guys did wind up staying in the Bay area. As one could imagine, I was quite ecstatic about that. Heck, Luke even went home with me for Thanksgiving and Christmas. He also found time to fly back to Florida so he could visit his family.

It was mid-afternoon and the winter semester just started. I was in my apartment diligently working on my homework, or at least pretending to be, when Alexa came around the corner. Her hair was up and she was in sweats.

"Hey, do you want to see if the guys want to go out tonight?"

I looked at her as I tried to comprehend the question.

"They'll be heading off to spring training soon so we need to monopolize our time as much as possible."

I liked where her head was.

"Do you think they'll be free tonight?"

Alexa dramatically threw her hands into the air.

"C'mon, Pam! What could they possibly be doing tonight that's soo important that they can't see us? It's not like they have any studying to do!"

She did have a point.

Alexa walked over, put her coffee cup onto my desk, and

whipped out her phone.

Luke Fisher

Julio and I were both sprawled out in our living room. He was on the couch while I was comfortably relaxing on the recliner. Julio picked up his phone.

"Well, it looks like we're being beckoned."

Unlike Pam and Alexa, my choice of drink for lazy afternoons was strawberry water, which I took a sip of before answering.

"Oh yeah? How so?"

"So I quote, 'us girls want to go out tonight.'" Julio paused. "That sounds like a demand to me."

I smiled. "Yeah...yeah it does."

I looked at the wall clock, but the batteries were dead. It was stuck at 1:26.

"You know, we really need to get new batteries for that damn clock."

Julio looked at the clock and smiled. What could he say? I was right.

Since the wall clock was of no help, Julio looked at his phone for the time.

"What about 7? That'll give them time to get ready."

As comfortable as we were lounging in our spots, we knew we didn't have a choice in the matter if we knew what was best for us. After all, we would be heading off to Arizona in a few weeks for spring training.

"I'm sure the girls will be up for a burger. What about that one place in downtown Palo Alto…I believe it's called *The Crazy Burger?*"

"Yeah, I've seen that place, but we've never eaten there. Sounds good to me. Check with the Generals."

Across the room I watched as Julio's fingers went to work on his phone.

Pam Thomson

A few minutes had passed by when all of sudden an "eeek" came from across the room.

"Do we have dates tonight?"

Alexa smiled. "Damn right, girl!" she said waving her index finger back and forth. "Julio suggested *The Crazy Burger* as a place to go."

"*The Crazy Burger*…ooooh…I've heard great things about that place."

Alexa enthusiastically stood up from the couch and quickly walked into her room.

"Oh hey, tell them they are staying the night as well." I said with a smile.

Alexa came back into my room with a smirk on her face.

"Isn't that a given?"

"Probably, but it doesn't hurt to give them a little reminder once in a while," I added.

Alexa smiled.

"Pam, you're so evil."

"Well, I just don't want them to wonder, you know. Sometimes we just have to smack them over the head with what we want."

Alexa turned and walked away with a smile on her face. I hope I wasn't too much of a bad influence on her.

Luke Fisher

I knocked on the door. There was a momentary silence until I heard someone fiddling with the door from the inside.

Pam swung the door open, and as always, her beauty floored me. She looked as beautiful then as she did the first time I saw her! I loved the way her long hair flowed midway down her back. Of course, she looked amazing in her jeans. Though she didn't always wear heels, when she did she was lights out. Hell, she even looked awesome when she wore sweats and a tank top! Yeah, I was one lucky guy. In addition, she was an economics major. Yeah, it just wasn't fair!

Pam lunged towards me and gave me a big hug.

"Hey, babe! How are you doing?"

I kissed her on the lips and playfully smacked her butt.

"Great to see you."

Pam pressed her right hand against my chest. She looked at me and smiled then turned her head to her right.

"Hey, Julio! How are you doing?"

Pam turned and guided us into the apartment. Alexa came around the corner and enthusiastically hugged Julio. As always, Alexa also looked amazing.

I was so proud to have Pam by my side wherever I went and I know Julio felt the same. Not only were they beautiful ladies, but they were both supportive, happy, and smart.

18

Coach Jacobs

Mid March

It was an uneventful holiday season. Julio and Alexa found time to stop by and visit with me while they were home for the holidays, which was nice. It was good to see them. Spring had arrived and it couldn't have come fast enough. Jeremy was so ready, as were a lot of us. I think he could've chewed through wood if given the opportunity. Every few days he would stop by and talk baseball. A number of the players, with Jeremy's lead, showed up before school to throw as well.

I was at the kitchen table sipping coffee and eating a bagel when my phone buzzed. It was Alexa!

Good luck this season! Bring home the championship!

It must have been five in the morning back in California. Her text made my day!

Not long after that morning text from Alexa, I drove across town to work. I wanted to get to school early so I could prepare for the day. It was, afterall, the beginning of a new baseball season.

As usual, the gym was quiet, which allowed me to get

some work done. Suddenly, I heard a loud knock on my office door. A little startled, I looked up. Jeremy was in the middle of the doorway smiling from ear to ear.

"Hey, bud. I see someone is ready for baseball to start!"

He didn't say a word. Instead, he just came in and sat down in his usual chair.

Again I asked, "Are you ready for the season?"

"Coach, I can't believe you're asking me that."

I had coached Jeremy for the previous three years and in that time I had never seen him so happy, outside of winning some big games of course.

He clapped his hands together enthusiastically.

"C'mon, Coach! Baseball is about to start!"

He paused.

"Well Coach, I know you're busy. I just wanted to say good morning to you on this glorious day."

I smiled. "Well, I'm glad you did."

Later in the day I passed through the hall towards the office. Five feet from the office door, I stopped because I heard my name.

"Coach! Hey Coach!"

I turned to my left, curious who was calling my name. I smiled when I saw Brandy waving her arms at me. She was in heels which made running a slight challenge. Not to mention her bag, which was full of books, was slung over her right shoulder.

"Hey. How are you? Are you okay?"

Slightly out of breath, she threw her arms around me.

"Over the weekend I received an email from CIU. I'll be earning a full academic scholarship next year!"

"That's awesome," though I'm not sure my response fully indicated how excited I was for her.

"I did it, Coach! I actually did it!" she exclaimed.

At that moment I was reminded why I taught. I was so proud of her.

"Have you told Jeremy yet?"

I expected to hear "yes" as the answer. They were dating and best friends after all.

She paused for a second and the smile left her face. I could see tears forming in her eyes. She stepped back and wiped her eyes with the back of her hand. She shook her head somberly.

"Why haven't you told him?"

"I'm not sure. I guess I want to wait for the right time."

She shrugged her shoulders as she continued to wipe her tears away with the back of her hands.

"Brandy, there's never the perfect time. I just know he would love to hear the news. Now get to class."

She wiped her eyes again.

"Yes sir."

She turned and walked in the opposite direction.

The rest of the day passed by rather quickly. Finally, the school day ended and baseball was about to begin. Most of the unknown players were freshmen, but I was even familiar with some of them. In a small town like Franklin, the good players made their mark early on. Little league dads pretending to be coaches would stop me in the grocery store and tell me about the next phenom. Before Don's untimely death, I would often refer those parents to him. Word quickly got out when I got the head coaching job though, and I had to hear from those same parents.

The first practice went smoother than expected. Coach Collins, my new assistant, rotated from station to station. Even though he did not teach at the high school, his rapport with the players was evident.

At one point Jeremy got on one of the younger players, which pleased me. I looked at Coach Collins and smiled.

Once practice finished, Jeremy quickly drove home. Not long after he was home, he received a text from Brandy.

Can you come over tonight?

Is everything okay?

Sure, I have something to share with you

He quickly ate dinner and excused himself from the table. Curiously, his dad looked at him.

"Where are you going in such a toot?"

"Oh, I'm heading to Brandy's. She has something to tell me."

"She's not going to break up with you, is she?" Mr. James asked jokingly.

"Geeze, I hope not."

"Mr. James!" his mom barked.

Several minutes later, he arrived at Brandy's house. He was glad to see Cali's car in the driveway as well. Surely she wouldn't break up with him with her cousin present.

Jeremy walked around to the back of the house. Cali and Brandy were in their respective porch chairs sipping their warm drinks. It was, after all, still rather chilly outside.

"Hello ladies!" Jeremy declared when he noticed them.

Brandy waved at Jeremy enthusiastically, while Cali whistled and yelled, "Well look who's here."

Brandy jumped from her chair and reached out for a hug.

"I couldn't wait to see you tonight!" she said after kissing him on the cheek.

Of course Cali yelled, "Get a room!"

Brandy turned towards Cali. "Oh, you're just jealous."

Cali laughed. "You're so right Cuz!"

Jeremy plopped down next to Brandy. She reached for his

left hand, which was resting on his leg. He looked at her curiously.

Brandy's upper lip began to quiver and her eyes began to well up with tears. Jeremy, concerned, looked at Cali who shook her head confusingly.

Jeremy looked back at Brandy. He opened his mouth to speak, but was interrupted. She raised her index finger to his mouth to silence him. She tapped his hand on her right leg several times.

"I...I...I just wanted to tell you, I've earned a full academic scholarship to CIU," she said with a weak smile.

Cali quietly clapped her hands.

Jeremy looked at Cali and then back at Brandy. She unsuccessfully hid her tears of joy. Afterall, it had been a long year for Brandy and her emotions were getting the best of her. Upset she was in tears, Jeremy put his arms around her.

"I'm so proud of you!"

She leaned into him and rested her head on his shoulder. The tears she worked to hide poured from her eyes as if the stress from the year had been lifted from her shoulders. Jeremy squeezed her as tight as he could and kissed her on her head several times.

"I'm so proud of you!" he repeated.

Cali wiped her eyes with a handful of tissues.

"Thank you, Jeremy. Thank you," Brandy said as she

cried.

"Just three more months and we're out of this dump," she whimpered.

Jeremy squeezed her again.

"If we can make it to State, the four years would be topped."

Brandy sat up. She looked at him and smiled.

"What do you mean 'if'? there's no 'if'. You're going to make it to State. I know it."

Cali raised her hands and happily yelled, "Can I get an 'amen'?!"

"That's right. You tell him Cali!" Brandy said with a smile.

19

Luke Fisher
Mid March

I couldn't believe another spring training was coming to a close. Even more amazing, it was Julio's and my second year in Arizona. Time sure had a way of flying by back then. For some reason, I was given a Friday afternoon off. Don't get me wrong, I wasn't complaining, I was just surprised.

I had been hitting the ball hard and working tirelessly to improve my swing and fielding, so I guess I earned it. I did go in early that day to hit in the cages, otherwise it just wouldn't have felt right.

Julio, on the other hand, had to throw seventy-five pitches and run a couple of miles. Yeah, I was glad I wasn't a pitcher. I did run and lift almost every day, but not nearly as much as the pitchers.

The location of our training camp was just beautiful! Mountains could be seen in the distance and on most days there weren't many clouds. It was the perfect place to work out, play games, or just relax after a hard day on the ball field, which is what I was doing that particular Friday afternoon.

I settled in on the couch with a glass of strawberry water in my hand. The TV was on in the background even though I wasn't paying much attention to what was on. I was startled when I heard a loud bang at the door.

"What the... who could that be?" I mumbled frustratingly as I nearly spilled my glass of water. I was comfortably relaxing on the couch after all! The audacity!

"Who is it?" I yelled. Yeah, I wasn't happy!

Again.

Bang! Bang! Bang!

I looked at the TV and then the door. Damn, I didn't want to get up!

"One moment!" I yelled frustratingly.

Pam Thomson

Neither I or Alexa had ever been to Arizona, much less to spring training to see our men. When Luke informed me they would be at their Arizona home for the weekend and not be traveling, and we realized we didn't have any tests in the near future, the wheels started churning in our heads.

Alexa came up with the idea. Not me. But I wish I had thought of it.

Alexa and I looked at each other and nearly started to laugh when we heard Luke carry on inside the apartment. I even had to cover my mouth. I nearly lost it.

Finally, the door swung open. Luke stood in the middle of the doorway in a pair of shorts with a glass of water in his hand. I tried to be healthy, but he definitely took it to another level.

"What the?!" he said in disbelief.

"SURPRISE!!!" Alexa And I exclaimed in tandem.

Luke didn't respond.

I lunged forward and gave Luke a hug. He still didn't say anything.

"Are you okay?" I asked. I quickly felt unwelcomed.

"No, I'm fine." He mumbled. "C'mon in...I'm just a little surprised. That's all."

I looked at Alexa and then Luke.

"Well, we've never been down here and we wanted to see you one more time before the season started."

"Yeah!" Alexa added.

She was clearly allowing me to be the spokesperson.

"How did you guys know where we live?"

I bit my lower lip and looked at Alexa.

"Umm... you wanna tell him?"

Alexa looked at me with her devilish grin.

"I asked Julio's parents for the address. Sorry."

Luke looked at me and then Alexa.

"No biggie. I was just curious... Make yourself at home." He looked around. "Damn, we would've had this place cleaned up had we known you were coming.

Alexa picked up a pair of sweats that were spread across the recliner and looked at them.

"Are these yours?"

Luke laughed.

"Um, nope. Those belong to Julio."

Alexa giggled.

"Not surprised."

She threw down the sweats and plopped herself in the recliner.

"Ahh, now this is nice."

I don't know why, but I awkwardly stood in the middle of the living room. Maybe I was waiting for Luke to tell me to sit down or something. I don't know.

Luke looked up at me.

"What are you doing? Sit down and relax."

I turned my upper body and looked at him. My arms were crossed. I guess I was hoping for a more enthusiastic greeting.

"No, I don't want to..." I muttered.

"C'mon, Pam! Sit down and relax," Alexa chimed.

After pouting for a minute or two and looking like a complete fool while doing it, I sat down next to Luke.

He put his arm around me and kissed my forehead.

"Glad you're here," he whispered.

I rested my head against his chest.

"Thanks."

After some time passed, I looked across the room. Much to my surprise, Alexa was out like a rock.

I smiled.

"She must be tired." I paused. "When will Julio be getting home?"

Luke looked at his phone for the time.

"He should be home shortly. All he had to do was run and throw some this afternoon."

Luke kissed me again on my head.

"Sorry if you thought I wasn't excited to see you. I'm just tired and I was surprised. That's all."

Even though he didn't need to apologize, I did appreciate it.

I slowly nestled comfortably into the couch. I was nearly asleep when the door sprung open. Startled, Alexa nearly fell out of her chair.

Julio walked in and immediately noticed things were different.

"Surprise!" I said with a smile.

Alexa was trying to wake up and gather her senses.

Julio looked at me, then Alexa, and then Luke.

Luke grinned.

"Don't look at me. I didn't know they were coming either."

Julio dropped his bags at the door. I could tell he was tired. He walked over to Alexa and kissed her on the forehead. Alexa was still pretty groggy, but she grinned when he kissed her.

"So how was your workout?" Luke asked as if Alexa and

I weren't there.

Julio sat on the couch with a thud.

"Tiring, but good. How was yours?"

Luke smiled.

"It was good, BUT not as tiring as yours, I'm sure."

Julio looked at Alexa.

"So when did you guys come in?"

"We got here about an hour ago or so." she responded in between yawns.

"Well, I'm hungry. What about you guys?"

He looked at Luke, Alexa, and then me. It was as if he was expecting us. Who knows? Maybe his parents told him to be expecting company.

After some deliberation we finally decided on a place to eat. Thankfully, none of us were picky when it came to food, unlike those annoying couples that can never decide on a place to eat.

Luke Fisher

I rolled over as my alarm buzzed obnoxiously. I had no desire to get out of bed. It was Sunday morning afterall and the clock read 6:00. Pam and Alexa had a flight to catch even though it wasn't for a few hours. Pam's head was on my chest which made it more than difficult to roll over and turn off the alarm. Somehow I did it without disturbing her.

After I slammed the snooze button, I rolled back over and kissed her on the head. She softly tapped me on the chest as she let out a soft grunt.

"Is that Alexa and Julio in the kitchen?" Pam asked as she laid in my bed like a slug.

I gently kissed her head again.

"Yep.t is."

"Geeze! I love those two, but they make me sick."

I smiled.

"Why's that?"

"Oh, they're just so perfect for each other."

I rubbed her shoulder with my right arm.

"So you don't think we're perfect for each other?"

She thumped me lovingly on the chest.

"Shut up. You know what I mean."

After a few more quiet minutes in bed, I kissed her again on the head.

"Well, I guess we better get up."

Pam and I slowly walked into the kitchen where Alexa and Julio were eating breakfast.

"Morning guys!" Alexa exclaimed.

Neither of us answered.

Pam shuffled her feet across the floor like a sixty year old man while I sauntered in behind her. I couldn't help but wonder why Alexa was so awake.

"Morning guys," Julio said as he took a sip of his coffee.

Pam walked by him towards the coffee maker.

"Morning," she grunted.

Julio looked at Pam and smiled followed by a look in my direction.

I tapped Julio on the shoulder while passing him towards the coffee maker.

"Yeah...Yeah, I know."

Pam took a sip of her coffee.

"So opening day is in a few weeks?"

"Yep," Julio immediately responded before I had a chance to say anything. "We have about two more weeks to go."

"It's about time you guys get back to San Fran," Alexa added.

I looked at Alexa.

"Yeah… We'll be back soon enough."

Both Alexa and Pam smiled.

Before long Alexa and Pam were both dressed and ready to go. Minutes later their cab arrived and they were gone.

Julio looked at me.

"Well... time to get to work."

We closed the door to the apartment and got dressed. It was time to prepare for the last few weeks of spring training.

20

Luke Fisher

Late March

It was three days before the end of spring training. Thank God, because I was ready to get the season underway. As much as I loved the Arizona mountains, the San Francisco mountains were equally beautiful and the weather wasn't nearly as harsh during the summer in San Francisco.

Me, Julio, and a couple of our teammates were sitting in the locker room playing cards at one of the tables when Coach Smith appeared in his office doorway.

"Julio, can we have a talk?" he yelled from across the locker room.

Julio laid down his cards.

"Sorry guys. I'm being called."

He took a deep breath then stood up.

Inside Coach Smith's office sat Coach Sims, the pitching coach. This was not uncommon.

Julio walked into the office and was then asked to shut the door.

Me and the other guys continued to play cards, but I couldn't help but wonder what they were discussing. Could Julio be traded? Would he be asked to start the season off in the bullpen? Would he be one of the starters? They were all possibilities. I, for one, was nervous for him. At the same time, I learned early on everyone was expendable -- even your friends.

About fifteen minutes after entering the office, Julio stood up. He opened the office door and exited. His shoulders weren't slumped which was a good thing, but I couldn't tell from his face if the conversation went well or not.

He refused to make eye contact with me and the other guys when he pulled his chair closer to the table, which made me more curious.

I glanced at Julio and then my cards. I wanted to ask him how the meeting went, but I didn't want to be too nosey. We were professionals after all and this was our job, so it was really none of my business what they discussed. It wasn't like I immediately told him I would be the starting centerfielder either.

After several minutes, Julio stood up.

"Well guys, I'm done for the day."

He wasn't very good at playing cards. As hard as he tried, he just never got the hang of it.

He quietly walked over to his locker and began to put on his uniform.

I looked at the wall clock.

"Yeah, I guess it's time to get dressed."

We had just two more scrimmage games left and both of

them were in the afternoon. It was ten in the morning, so like Julio, I excused myself from the table to get my uniform on. Most of the guys had left the locker room for the field by the time I was finished getting dressed. I was in the process of tying my last shoe when a pair of shoes appeared in my line of sight. I looked up and there stood Julio.

Unlike before, he had a grin on his face.

"I'll be starting the opening game on Monday," he said as he continued to smile.

I stopped tying my shoe and sat up. I grinned and nodded my head.

"Well nice job bud! I'm excited for you!"

Julio continued to smile as he left the locker room.

I looked around the room and noticed I was one of the last ones to leave. So I reached into my locker and grabbed my phone.

Julio is starting on Opening Day!

Pam immediately responded.

Yay! That's so exciting!

A moment passed before I got another text.

Does Alexa know?

I responded immediately.

I don't know, he was just told this morning!

Pam quickly responded.

I'll let her know! She'll be excited!

She continued...

I can't wait to see you

Well I got to go, luv you

Before I had a chance to see her response, I put my phone away and headed out the door towards the field.

21

Coach Jacobs

Early April

The players hustled down to the field as soon as the bell rang. The team was ready for it's first game after a horrendous season the year before. The seniors were especially excited. The first game of the year was against one of our traditional opponents. As much as we would've liked to have played some competition in the beginning, a team like Clariton was always a nice way to start the season. They weren't well coached nor were their players very talented. In a nutshell, the game would be a win for us as long as we didn't give them the game.

Jeremy was evidently excited. He walked up and down the dugout and yelled at his teammates, which slightly surprised me and Coach Collins. I was glad to see Jeremy's leadership.

The crowd was small. I wasn't terribly surprised because the temperatures were a little chilly. Chilly temperatures and poor competition usually meant a small turnout. Thankfully, the sun was out and there was no wind.

"You ready to whoop some butt?!" a voice yelled out.

There was silence.

"Coach! Are you ready to whoop some butt?!"

I looked to my right and Jeremy was walking towards me. His catcher's gear covered him. He looked like a knight ready to go into battle. With no luck, I tried to hide my smile. His enthusiasm was electric.

After the pregame conference with the coach from Clariton and the two umpires, I turned towards the dugout and motioned to the players. Quietly, the players filed out of the dugout and walked towards the first base line. A silence fell upon the bleachers. Those who weren't paying attention were nudged by their friends to stand. We all looked towards the right field corner and watched as Kyle's and Coach Wilson's numbers were unveiled. With little success, Brandy tried to hide her tears. Cali leaned over and gave her a hug. Like Jeremy, my eyes welled up with tears.

As he stared towards the outfield, a butterfly danced around him. Jeremy thought about the one he saw at Jamie's gravestone the previous summer.

After ten seconds of silence, Jeremy looked to the sky.

"This year is for you, Kyle."

As for me, I stood with my hands on my hips in silence. The whole time I looked down. I guess I didn't want anyone to see that I was crying because I missed my friend.

In a sprint, Jeremy led the starters onto the field while the subs jogged back into the dugout. Brandy clapped enthusiastically after she wiped the tears from her eyes. Down the right field line beyond the fence stood Jeremy's parents.

Kory, the starting pitcher, stepped onto the mound. He

zipped the ball towards home plate harder than ever before. It was evident Kory had worked hard the past few years to improve his fastball. After the first three batters for Clariton made outs, Jeremy hustled in like he always did.

"Coach, they're not going to hit Kory. He's cheesin the ball."

I overheard one of the freshmen ask another player, "what's cheesin mean?" The other one replied, "he's throwing hard, you idiot," obviously aggravated he had to answer such a simple question.

I couldn't help but smile.

In five innings the game was over because we scored ten on them, while Kory didn't allow any runs on two hits. Jeremy hit the ball every time he was up. It was a nice victory.

The next few games went well. It felt good to beat up on our opponents after the previous year we had. The team played like they had something to prove. I was also glad to see two of our younger pitchers, Josh and Tommy, throw well.

The days slowly warmed as we approached the middle part of our schedule. Jeremy would pass me in the hall every day and yell enthusiastically, "Coach, you ready for another victory?!"

The day before our game against Carbondale, Jeremy, along with Brandy, saw me in the hall.

"Coach!" he yelled, "Are we going to beat Carbondale

tomorrow?!”

Never the vocal coach, I simply nodded my head and smiled.

“Coach!” he replied, “Show more enthusiasm than that!”

Later that night after practice, Jeremy went over to Brandy’s house. Though it was in the low forties, they somehow sat outside under the stars.

For once, it was just them. Cali was off doing her thing with golf. It had been eight months since Coach had died and around a year since Kyle and Jamie had died.

“Hey Jer...are you excited about college?”

“Yeah, though honestly I’m hoping to leave my mark here at Franklin before I go.” He paused. “I’ll never be Julio, but I want to be remembered as one of those players, you know?”

Brandy squeezed Jeremy with her arms and kissed his shirt covered chest.

“Well, you’ll always be tops in my book.” Silence filled the air. “Besides, you have achieved so much more than him.”

Jeremy was immediately perplexed.

“Oh yeah? How so?”

She looked at him sternly.

“Well duh, he was only here for two years, while you have lived in this racist God forsaken town for four years. You’ve won state and you’ve overcome the deaths of several friends.”

He leaned over and kissed her forehead.

"Well... I hope we can make it to State and the rest would be icing on the cake."

Brandy tapped Jeremy on the stomach.

"What do you mean 'if'? No 'if' about it mister. You WILL make it to State." She paused. "Have you talked to your brother lately?"

He didn't immediately answer her.

"We talked yesterday. I guess things are going well in San Fran. Alexa is also doing well." He paused again. "Damn, it's hard to believe she's finishing up her second year at Stanford."

"Wow, time sure does fly."

"I wonder if that will be us in a few years." Again he paused. "Well, I know one thing. We have Carbondale tomorrow, so I better get home," he said begrudgingly.

Brandy pretended to pout even though she totally understood and appreciated his devotion to the game he loved so much.

"Well if you have to go... I'll be there cheering you on, sweetie. Love you."

22

Coach Jacobs

Mid April

The bus rolled up to Carbondale's field and stopped fifteen feet away from the dugout. Jeremy sat in the same spot up near the front of the bus for the last three years. He never seemed to have any inclination to move to the back with the other guys. I guess some people are just creatures of habit.

I glanced at the team. I was about to speak when I looked at Jeremy.

"Hey Coach, how about we get off this bus and go kick some Carbondale butt?" he said quietly.

Several of his teammates somehow heard him and yelled their support.

I thought I would give some inspirational words of encouragement. Apparently they had no desire to listen to me. At the end of the day, I guess I didn't blame them. Without so much as a 'let's go', I proceeded to walk off the bus.

For some reason, both Coach Collins and I were worried. Neither of us knew why. We just were. It didn't help that minutes before the game Jeremy walked into the dugout after he and Kory got done loosening up. He looked at me nervously.

"How's Kory looking?" Coach Collins asked.

I guess Coach Collins didn't see Jeremy's facial que or he just didn't know him well enough.

"He looks fine, Coach," Jeremy replied.

Coach Collins nudged me.

"I have a feeling this isn't going to be Kory's day."

Taped on the dugout wall was my roster and lineup.

"Shit, I just hope Kory can get through five innings," I replied.

The Carbondale team ran onto the field to mark the start of the game. Even though they were not loaded with talent, the team was always scary to play. In a word, they were "scrappy." Our first three batters went up to bat and made three straight outs. It wasn't the start we had hoped for.

The bottom half of the inning didn't go so well for us either. Unlike our batters, the Carbondale players hit the ball hard from the start. Every out was a struggle for Kory. The inning finally came to a close, but Carbondale had scored four runs.

Jeremy was visibly upset when he arrived in the dugout. He paced back and forth and yelled at his teammates. Kory stood at the far end of the dugout. I could tell he was frustrated.

The second and third innings didn't fare much better for us. Even though Kory was throwing the ball hard and his curve seemed to be working, they hit him like it was batting practice.

We couldn't buy a run either. Even when we had runners in scoring position we were unsuccessful.

Tommy replaced Kory in the fourth inning. We hoped a lefty could slow down the Carbondale batters. Sadly, they kept hitting the ball. The game couldn't end fast enough. Finally, the fifth inning arrived. They scored a few more in the fifth to beat us by ten. Losing by the slaughter rule really stunk!

Jeremy walked off the field with his head down. He wasn't the only player who appeared upset or disappointed.

The bus ride home was indeed a quiet one. The older players made sure of that. Coach and I looked at each other several times, but neither of us could muster up the energy to talk about the game. We just shook our heads in disgust. This was one of those games we wanted to quickly forget.

Later that evening Jeremy drove over to Brandy's house. He laid on her porch couch with his head on her lap.

"Well, the season is far from over," he mumbled.

Brandy listened while she ran her fingers across his chest.

"I mean, we still have Vienna and Cartersville in a week and even then there's the regional tournament."

Brandy opened her mouth, but held back from saying anything. She just nodded her head. After what she had seen earlier in the day, she wasn't terribly optimistic.

23

Coach Jacobs

Late April

The last thing I wanted was a cold front to move in. Well, the afternoon Vienna came to town turned out to be one of those days. As the day rolled on, I continuously checked the weather on my computer. I hoped for a warm front to miraculously come in, but I knew better.

School finally ended for the day. I wanted to be excited about the game because we were playing one of the best teams in the region, but the thought of standing in nearly freezing temperatures and blustery cold wind didn't excite me one bit. It made me cold just thinking about it. Luckily, us Coaches had the luxury of layering up with clothes unlike the players who weren't so lucky.

Coach Collins was in the dugout when I arrived. The poor guy looked like a marshmallow because he had so many layers on.

"Hey Coach, are you a little cold?"

He looked at me with disgust.

Eventually the players, one by one, began trickling into the dugout. Some were dressed warmer than others. Jeremy brought his gear into the dugout and plopped it down nearest to home plate.

"Hey Coach, it's a little cold out here, don't you think?"

"Yes...yes it is," I replied.

Eventually the Vienna bus rumbled up to the field. Jeremy seemed especially focused. At one point he looked at Josh who was slated to pitch.

"One thing you have going for you today is the wind. Shoot, look at that wind blowing in from centerfield."

Josh looked over his left shoulder towards the flags. His jaw dropped.

"Shit, those flags are blowing straight in," he said with amazement.

Baffled, Tommy looked at Josh.

"You didn't notice that before now? You're an idiot."

Normally, the game against Vienna would attract droves of fans from both towns, but the numbers were much smaller because it was cold and windy. Brandy was one of the few dedicated fans... or she was crazy. Not sure which.

One would have never known it was her because her scarf covered her face. She was also wearing a stocking cap, gloves, multiple layers of sweatshirts, and a huge puffy black coat. She looked like a layered up ninja. I knew it was her simply because she sat in the same spot for every game the last two years. Otherwise, I would have never guessed.

Thankfully, the game flew by. Both teams were actually pretty evenly matched. Josh gained an extra five miles per hour on his fastball because of the wind. To add to the torment, every time a batter made contact their hands would sting. In the fourth inning, with the score tied at one, Jeremy blooped one into right field. When he reached first, Jeremy screamed in pain. As a last resort, he shoved his hands down his pants for warmth. The players on the bench, of course, couldn't help but tease him-- even though they would've done the same damn thing.

By the sixth inning, the game remained tied at one. Shawn Smith, who was now in relief for Josh, threw the ball up near ninety miles per hour. Shawn had become one of our main relievers. He was able to get the Vienna batters out rather quickly.

At the end of the inning, Jeremy came into the dugout in agony because the pitches were stinging his hand.

"Is he throwing hard?" Coach Collins asked sarcastically.

"What do you think, Coach? Look at my hand!"

The first batter up for us in the bottom of the sixth was Keith Smith. He was a scrappy left fielder with lightning speed. In four pitches, the pitcher walked him. The next batter up was Marc Jones followed by Jeremy. All we needed was one run. With Shawn in relief, I had no doubt we'd win the game.

As Marc approached home, I called time. He stepped away from home plate and looked at me. He noticed me walking towards him. I could tell he wasn't excited about the mini meeting because he slumped his shoulders.

I approached him and whispered, "I want you to bunt. All we need is one run."

He never made eye contact with me. Instead, he looked towards our dugout. He walked back to home plate and stepped up to hit. Prior to the pitch, he squared up to bunt. The pitch was perfect to bunt, which he did. He just advanced the winning runner to second.

Jeremy walked up to the plate. The few fans we had stood up and cheered. Brandy jumped up and down enthusiastically. The first pitch to Jeremy was outside for ball one. He stepped off the plate and looked towards me. He stepped back up to the plate after taking a deep breath. The next pitch was perfectly thrown, as it curved out off the plate. Jeremy swung and missed the pitch by a mile for a strike. Jeremy stepped out of the batter's, took another breath, shook his head in disgust, and stepped back up to hit.

Brandy watched nervously.

The count was one ball and one strike. The pitcher paused on top of the mound. He looked back towards the runner on second and threw the pitch home.

CLANK!

Jeremy hit the ball!

The Franklin fans jumped up and frantically yelled.

The ball whistled into left center field. Keith paused at

second to ensure the ball would drop and not be caught. As soon as he noticed the ball drift past the shortstop, he took off like a rocket towards third base. Half-way down the third base line, I swung my right arm frantically. Keith sprinted around third in full stride towards home. The centerfielder charged in on the ball. As Keith passed me, I could see the ball zoom in from centerfield. From my vantage point I thought he was going to be thrown out, but the wind worked in our favor. The ball sailed over the catcher's head as Keith slid into home. We were up by one!

Brandy jumped up and down in a circle as she looked for someone to hug. I looked out towards second base and noticed Jeremy pumping his fist excitedly. The momentum was now clearly in our favor. I motioned for Tom Jackson, our next batter, to swing away.

Tom confidently stepped up to bat. Two pitches went by for balls. The count was two balls and no strikes. The pitcher had no desire to put another runner on base, which is why the pitcher threw the next pitch down the middle of the plate. Tom lined the ball down the third base line. As soon as the ball passed the third baseman, Jeremy took off towards third. He surprised me when I noticed he wasn't stopping at third. Instead he rounded third hard and headed towards home. I could tell he was determined to score. Somehow Jeremy slid under the catcher's tag to score. Again, another play at home in our favor! Jeremy sprung up after his slide into home and threw his arms into the air. Ecstatic, he looked towards the dugout and yelled enthusiastically. We were now up by two runs. Clearly enough for Shawn to shut the door on Vienna.

The wind continued to gust towards home plate as Shawn walked out towards the mound.

"Three more outs, Jeremy. That's all we need," I said emphatically as I passed him at home plate.

"We got this, Coach!" he replied confidently.

Thankfully, the bottom of the order was also due up. The first batter stepped in. To our advantage, the sun was now below the horizon, which dipped the temperature even closer to freezing. The first batter struck out on three pitches. I think he was actually afraid to hit the ball because it was so cold out. The last batter in the lineup came up to hit. He was equally weak at the plate. Shawn made quick work of him as well.

"All we need is one more out!" Coach yelled enthusiastically.

Brandy couldn't decide whether to stand up or sit down. She was so excited, but also cold. The bleachers rattled while Brandy and the others stomped their feet.

Shawn gathered his thoughts, took a breath, and stepped onto the rubber up on the mound for what he hoped would be strike three. He went into his windup and threw the ball home.

POP!

The ball hit Jeremy's glove and stung like a scorpion. Before the umpire even had a chance to call strike three, Jeremy leaped from his crouching position. Immediately after Jeremy jumped to his feet, the umpire yelled "STRIKE THREE!" which ended the game. Everyone in the dugout threw their arms into the air. The region rankings were now up in the air.

Brandy jumped down from the bleachers and ran towards the fence. She caught Jeremy's attention. He shyly waved at her. It was priceless.

One game down, one more to go. Now the Cartersville game was even more important.

24

Coach Jacobs
Late April

As I prepared for another day of work, Brandy showed up to school early and excited. It had been a couple of days since our victory against Vienna. She stood in the middle of my office doorway.

"Hey, Brandy. What's up?"

She walked in and sat down. I could tell by her mannerisms she was nervous about something.

Again I asked, "What can I do for you?"

She looked at me and then looked towards the corner of my office.

"Beat Cartersville tomorrow, Coach," she finally squeaked out as she looked at me.

I was humored and confused.

"Is that all you needed to talk about?"

"Yeah," she muttered. "I guess I'm just tired and ready for school to be done… and I'm sorry but I hate those S.O.Bs!"

Her frankness made me smile.

"Well, hang in there. We're in the home stretch. By the way, I saw you were at the game the other night. What did you think?"

"Oh man. It was painfully cold, but I was so proud of

Jeremy." She paused. "How do you think you'll do tomorrow?"

I could've answered with a bunch of coach speak mumble jumble, but instead I was curious what she thought.

"How do you think we'll do?"

"Oh man. You're asking me? Geeze. Uh, well, I think it will be a tough game." She paused and gently bit her upper lip. "I mean, I haven't seen Cartersville, but from what I've seen of our team, we can win. It just depends on which team shows up."

"What do you mean?"

"Well, if the Franklin team that beat Vienna shows up tomorrow, we'll win. If not... whew.. it may be a long game."

I smiled. Her insight was quite insightful and impressive.

"Well then, let's hope we play tomorrow like we did against Vienna."

I knew the time was nearing for the morning bell to ring. So did she.

"Well Coach, I should run. I just wanted to wish you good luck tomorrow."

Before I had a chance to respond, she was up and out the door. She looked back, smiled, and waved at me as she turned the corner.

The spring days seemed to go just a little quicker. Maybe because school was nearly out or because baseball kept me active and involved. Either way, Friday came to a close as quickly as it began. In less than twelve hours, we would be facing Cartersville.

The morning of the game was such a blur. I felt like I was in the tropics compared to the previous evening afternoon against Vienna.

Before the game I looked at Coach.

"Maybe the Vienna game was a turning point?"

Of course I was afraid of jinxing the team, so I made sure no one else on the team was around me.

Low and behold, Brandy was spot on. From the start, Cartersville never had a chance. Kory threw six strong innings and only allowed three hits. We scored runs like I hadn't seen before. Granted, we didn't win by ten, but when you handily beat a good team like Cartersville, it's a good victory. Proudly, our fans remained on their feet the whole game. A few times they were even obnoxiously loud. I guess, in the end, I didn't blame them.

The game finally came to a close. After we shook their hands, my players walked out to right field. I looked at Jeremy.

"Does it feel good to beat them?"

Jeremy glanced over his left shoulder towards the Cartersville team.

"IT FEELS AWESOME."

Behind me I could hear Brandy and a few other students

yell enthusiastically in our direction. Several players looked over their right shoulder and happily acknowledged them. Jeremy looked back and shook his head.

"You'd think we've never won before, Coach," he said embarrassingly.

I put my left arm over Jeremy's shoulder.

"Embrace it, bud. No one can take this away from you."

Jeremy shook his head.

"I know, but I want to win State."

"Well let's hit the home stretch and then go win State."

Jeremy looked at me and smiled.

"Sounds good, Coach."

25

Luke Fisher
Early June

Another season was underway here in San Francisco. After Julio's opening day outing, which the team won, the team continued to play well. He actually won all seven of the games he started going into June. Yeah, the guy was dominating the league.

Julio and I were enjoying one of our few mornings off because we had a late game. Both Alexa and Pam were at the apartment when Julio's phone rang unexpectedly.

I could tell the news was good, but I wondered who the heck he was talking to. Finally, he hung up the phone and looked at me with a smile.

"Jeremy's team is going to State!" he said proudly.

I thought back to my days in high school and happily reminisced about my team advancing to State.

Suddenly, a squeal came from the bathroom.

"Julio! Julio! Jeremy's team is going to State!"

Seconds later, Alexa came sprinting around the corner of the apartment. The whole time she was struggling to pull up her pants. She was so excited about the news she didn't even fully dress herself prior to exiting the bathroom.

Out of breath from her quick sprint through the

apartment, she stopped in the kitchen.

"Did you not hear me?!" she exclaimed. "Jeremy's team is going to State!"

Julio and I looked at each other as if we didn't care.

Pam, ever the buzz kill, chimed in.

"They know, Alexa. They're just being mean."

Coach Jacobs

The first game in State was a nail biter against the northern Illinois perineal power, Oswego. Amazingly, we won! Mentally tired, I slowly walked to right field to talk to the team. By the time I reached the team, they were all on one knee. I took a deep breath.

"Guys, this is just one game, but let me remind you the route we took was a bumpy one. Remember who you are playing for. As Coach Wilson used to say, 'all gravel roads lead to roads paved.' I want you to think about that for a moment." I paused. "In each of your lives there are going to be challenges. It's how you come out on the other end that defines you. Again, good job guys, but we are far from our goal. We have several more games to go and it starts now."

After I finished talking to the team, I walked back towards the dugout. I stopped because I felt a nudge on my back.

"One down, Coach," laughed Jeremy.

After nudging me, he walked out of the dugout and

greeted Brandy with a hug.

Pam Thomson

Alexa fidgeted with her phone while she waited for the most current text from Brandy who was keeping her up to date with the score. As much as Julio wanted to be able to follow the game, he couldn't because of work. The second game neared the end when Alexa received a text.

Franklin losing by 2, uggg

A second text immediately followed.

1 inning left

In disgust, Alexa launched her phone across the living room. It nearly hit me by mistake. I dared not say anything to Alexa since I was kind of afraid of this side of her. She sat on the couch and waited impatiently for the next text. Finally, she jumped up and ran across the living room for her phone while I cowered in fear.

"Are you okay?" I asked, half scared.

In disgust, Alexa stopped in her tracks and looked at me.

"What!? Are you freaken kidding me?! We're down to Providence!"

How was I to know that?

A loud *ding* came from her phone.

Alexa hesitated, then looked at her phone.

"NO!"

Coach Jacobs

Somberly, the team walked to the middle of the field to shake hands with the players from Providence. Tears filled the eyes of numerous players. Several hung their heads in disappointment. After we worked through the line, the team walked slowly to right field. Though we made this walk a hundred times before, it seemed farther than ever before. At least for me it did.

I looked at the team huddled around me. I couldn't think of the proper words to tell the guys, but I tried.

"Guys, I just want to say thanks for the hard fought year. Think about the last two years and the challenges we've faced. This season was for Kyle and Coach. I think they would be proud of our accomplishments." My voice began to quiver. "Be proud of what you have done. I can't say how much you guys mean to me." I took another breath. "Seniors, I especially want to say thanks to you. We've been through a lot the last four years, but it's been an amazing ride."

Behind me I could hear some of the students yelling. At first, I couldn't make out what they were saying since my focus was on the team. Eventually, I was able to make out what several of the students were yelling and it tugged at my heart.

"Franklin, we love you!"

"You guys rock!"

"Keep your heads up!"

Of course, Brandy was the loudest or at least the most distinctive.

After I released the players, Jeremy stayed in the same spot where he was kneeling.

"You okay?"

Jeremy stood up and reached out with his hand. Tears were in his eyes. One lonely tear ran down his left cheek.

"Coach --Uhhh -- I just wanted to say thanks for all you have done the last few years."

Behind me I could hear Brandy yell for Jeremy.

"Jeremy, I love you...keep your head up. I want to thank you. Now go over and thank Brandy, will you?"

I threw my arms around him because I was so proud of him.

"You will go far. Farther than your brother," I whispered.

"Thanks, Coach," Jeremy whispered in return as tears continued to run down his face.

Jeremy slowly walked towards Brandy with his head down and his shoulders slumped. Beyond the fence, Brandy waited for him patiently.

26

Coach Jacobs

Early August

Jeremy sat comfortably in the back seat of his parents SUV as they zoomed down the interstate towards Central Illinois University. For an August day in Illinois, the temperature was slightly cooler than normal. Several vehicles zipped by them as if they were standing still. Not to be outdone, Jeremy's dad passed several vehicles as well. Jeremy's mind wandered, curious if the passengers in the respective cars contained college students like him heading towards Champaign or some other school.

Finally, the dorms and the football stadium appeared in the distance. As excited as he was, he was also quite nervous. So much so he felt a little queasy.

"Here you go, son. Your new home!" his dad announced proudly as they approached the outskirts of Champaign.

Jeremy meekly smiled.

Slightly overwhelmed, his eyes dashed from side to side. Mrs. James looked at Jeremy through her mirror and winked. One less mouth to feed in her house saddened her.

Jeremy's phone vibrated.

Where are you?

Jeremy smiled.

We're nearly there...we just entered Champaign

Across town Brandy smiled. Like Jeremy, she was excited about the new adventures to come. The last two years had been taxing on her.

The rest of the morning flew by. After several trips up and down the elevator, Jeremy was finally moved into his dorm. He was torn between wanting to see his parents leave versus them staying a little longer.

As he and his parents prepared to make their way down to the car, Jeremy felt his phone vibrate again.

What are you doing for lunch?

"Hey dad, Brandy is curious about what we're doing for lunch."

"She is, huh? Well how about we all meet somewhere?"

Always game for a free lunch, Jeremy didn't hesitate in his response.

"Sounds good. I'll give her a call."

After some deliberation, the two families finally decided to meet at the mall where several restaurants were located.

Somehow Jeremy and his parents beat Brandy's entourage, which consisted of her mom, dad, and Cali.

After exchanging hellos, the group slowly walked towards the mall. Lost in their own world, Brandy and Jeremy walked side by side through the doors of the mall.

"No way!" Cried Cali.

Surprised, Jeremy and Brandy looked at her.

"Leslie, is that you?!"

Simultaneously Jeremy and Brandy noticed a tall slender girl with long hair.

"Holy crap! Cali, why are you here?"

"Girl, I was going to ask you the same thing."

Cali lunged forward and gave Leslie a hug.

After hugging Leslie, Cali pointed towards Brandy and Jeremy.

"Leslie, this is my cousin Brandy and her boyfriend Jeremy. They'll be going to CIU this year."

"Get out of here!" Leslie declared as she looked at Brandy and Jeremy. "It's nice to meet you two. Any friend of Cali's is a friend of mine."

"How do you know Cali?" asked Brandy.

Leslie smiled.

"Oh. This girl and I competed on the golf course for several years against each other. She's a tough cookie."

Cali proudly smiled.

Leslie looked at Cali.

"It was nice to see you. Good luck this upcoming year. Maybe we'll run into each other on the golf course."

"Oh, you know we will!" Cali quickly responded.

The two families finally sat down for their lunch. Their lunch went quicker than Jeremy would've liked. Brandy was more excited to see her parents leave than he was.

As they walked towards their respective vehicles, Brandy looked at Jeremy.

"Call me when you're free, okay?"

Jeremy grinned and gave her a kiss.

"Will do."

After driving through Champaign, Jeremy's dad pulled into the parking lot nearest to his dorm. After dodging several cars, they slowly walked inside the dormitory and quietly rode the elevator up to his floor.

His parents knew Jeremy was ready for them to leave or at least they assumed so.

Once in the room, his dad reached out with his hand which contained two twenty dollar bills. "Son, we're so proud of you."

"Yes, we are," added his mom.

"Thanks, guys. I appreciate it."

After a quick hug from his mom and dad, he was all alone in the dorm.

He stood quietly in the middle of his room. After several minutes his phone vibrated. To his surprise it was his brother.

I'm proud of you Jer

Jeremy held up his phone and snapped a picture of his dorm room. He pressed send. Seconds later he received another text from Julio.

Wow that's awesome

Jeremy, overwhelmed with pride, began to cry.

Epilogue

6 years later

Luke Fisher

Late June

In the distance, I heard a deep voice yell my name just as I finished my batting practice.

"Hey, Luke! Get your butt over here!"

I looked around, unable to locate the person who yelled my name. Finally, I noticed Julio some twenty feet away from me with his arm around the shoulders of a Cub's player. For a moment I was puzzled because the player didn't immediately look familiar. Then it hit me. It's Julio's brother, Jeremy! It had been two years since he had been drafted by the Cubs. After a year and half in the minor leagues, he was finally in the majors as a backup catcher.

"Look! It's my little brother!" Julio proudly declared as he pounded his left hand on Jeremy's chest. It had been six years since I last saw him and man had he filled out. He was as big as Julio.

"Well, he doesn't look so small," I happily declared as I shook his hand. "So, are you going to get a hit off this guy?"

I playfully jabbed Julio with my elbow.

"Nah, man. I'm still coming off the bench."

"Well hang in there. You'll get your chance," I replied. "So is the family here?" I asked as I glanced around the semi empty stadium.

"Yeah, they wouldn't have missed this for anything," Julio proudly replied.

Coach Jacobs

Since I had never been to Wrigley Field, I was overcome with excitement. Having lived and worked in southern Illinois most of my life, a trip to Chicago was challenging enough. Not to mention I was a Cardinals fan. I immediately noticed the ivy on the outfield walls and the chilly evening temperature even though it was mid-summer.

Before I had a chance to speak, Alexa jumped up from her seat. If it wasn't for the baby in her arms, I believe she would've climbed over the people she was seated next to so she could get to me.

"Coach, it's so good to see you!" she exclaimed.

As she worked her way towards me, I noticed Jeremy and Julio's parents happily in their seats. Brandy was next to them. She looked much older and more mature from when I last saw her. Dang, where had the years gone?

The game remained scoreless until the fifth inning when the Cubs finally scored off Julio. In the sixth and seventh inning the Giants weren't able to score, but then again, it was hard not to cheer for the Cubs since Jeremy was on that team.

It was fun to watch Brandy and Alexa banter back and forth throughout the game.

As the eighth inning neared, I noticed the pitcher for the Cubs was due up to hit.

"Mr. James, I see the pitcher is due up. I wonder who the Cubs are going to use as a pinch hitter."

Mr. James looked at me curiously. I looked through my binoculars into the Cub's dugout.

"Well I'll be… Hey guys, you aren't going to believe this," I said with the binoculars pressed to my face.

Both Alexa and Brandy answered simultaneously.

"Believe what?"

I passed the binoculars on to Mr. James.

"Look towards the dugout, guys. You're never going to guess who's coming up to hit!"

Brandy sat up in her seat.

"What! Who?"

NEXT UP … PINCH HITTER … JEREMY JAMES blared from the loud speakers. As soon as his name was announced, a picture of Jeremy popped up on the big screen in centerfield.

Enthusiastically, everyone in our row jumped to our feet.

Pam Thomson

As nice as it would have been to be at the game, I had a

job. Not long after college, I was hired by a small investment firm in the San Francisco area utilizing my economics degree. Even though Luke made enough money for the both of us and our two year old daughter, I still wanted to work. My Stanford degree would have felt like a big ole fat waste otherwise. Besides, I actually wanted to work. I missed Luke when he and the team were away on their road trips, but between work and taking care of our daughter, Bella, I kept busy. My family lived fairly close if and when I needed help taking care of Bella, which was nice. When Alexa and I had free time, we could often be found together shopping, attempting to play tennis, which we started to play while in college, lounging by a pool, and of course playing with our kids. No matter what we were doing, coffee was always involved. Imagine that!

Luke Fisher

I laughed as Jeremy approached home plate. I couldn't believe it. I turned and looked up towards the big screen. Yep, it was him.

Jeremy dug his feet into the ground. I tried to focus on my job out in centerfield, but I couldn't wipe the grin from my face. Julio allowed his brother to come set before he went into his motion. The first pitch was released up and in. I couldn't believe it! Julio threw his little brother a pitch up and in. He couldn't have been trying to hit him! No way! I wished I was closer to the action. I had to enjoy it from afar, which was the next best thing.

The next pitch was thrown for a strike on the outside part of the plate. The two worked the count to three balls and two strikes. Julio momentarily stepped off the mound. He wiped his brow with his left arm and took a deep breath. He was a competitive dude so the last thing he wanted to do was give up a hit to his brother or much less walk him. A walk would be just as bad because he would have been accused of being afraid to pitch to his little brother by our teammates.

He stepped up onto the mound. He worked into his motion and released the pitch towards home.

SMACK!

Coach Jacobs

The final pitch was thrown.

SMACK!

The ball jumped off Jeremy's bat. Our row, along with everyone around us, jumped to our feet. We watched with amazement, joy, and excitement as the ball drifted towards centerfield and into the night sky.

The End

www.ingramcontent.com/pod-product-compliance
Lightning Source LLC
Chambersburg PA
CBHW060928050726
47592CB00003B/870